CW01663089

# COSY

Ed Adams

First published in Great Britain in 2023 by firstelement
Copyright © 2023 Ed Adams
Directed by thesixtwenty

10 9 8 7 6 5 4 3 2
All rights reserved.

No part of this publication may be reproduced, stored in a retrieval system, or transmitted, in any form or by any means, without the prior permission in writing of the publisher, nor be otherwise circulated in any form or binding or cover other than that in which it is published and without a similar condition including this condition being imposed on the subsequent purchaser.

Every effort has been made to acknowledge the appropriate copyright holders. The publisher regrets any oversight and will be pleased to rectify any omission in future editions.

Similarities with real people or events is unintended and coincidental.
A CIP catalogue record for this book is available from the British Library.

ISBN 13: 978-1-913818-34-0

eBook ISBN: 978-1-913818-35-7

Printed and bound in Great Britain by Ingram Spark

**rashbre**
**an imprint of firstelement.co.uk**
**rashbre@mac.com**

ed-adams.net

## *Thanks*

A big thank you for the tolerance and bemused support from all of those around me. To those who know when it is time to say, "step away from the keyboard!" and to those who don't.

To Julie for continued understanding.
To John, for hangin' in there
To Caroline, dafür, dass du mir etwas über die Drogenkultur beigebracht hast.
To thesixtwenty.co.uk for direction.
To the NaNoWriMo gang for the continued encouragement.
To those who provided inspiration at SPS London 2022.
To the London hotel which gave me a wonderful free room.
To Topsham, for being lovely.
To the edge-walkers. They know who they are.

And, to a few websites:

**Ed Adams Amazon Page:**
https://amzn.to/3NRPqXV

*Ed Adams Catalogues:*
https://ed-adams.net
https://ed-adams.mysites.io

*Rashbre blog:*
https://rashbre2.blogspot.com

Plus, the cast of amazing and varied readers whether human, twittery, smoky, artistic, cool kats, photographic, dramatic, musical, anagrammed, globalized, or maxed.

Not forgetting the cast of characters involved in producing this; they all have virtual lives of their own.

And of course, to you, dear reader, for at least 'giving it a go'.

## *Author's Note*

This is one in a collection of what started out as London-based crime thrillers featuring the characters of Jake, Clare, Bigsy, Christina Nott, Chuck Manners, and Amanda Miller.

Titles include, The Triangle, The Square, The Circle, Raven, Raven's Card, Archangel and Play On Christina Nott.

Now I've moved to the west country, the latest one is set around Exeter, and has more of a cosy crime feel to it.

Before the real Ed Adams twists kick in.

I hope you enjoy!

Ed

# *Ed Adams Novels*

| Triangle Trilogy | | About | Link |
|---|---|---|---|
| T1 | The Triangle | Dirty money? Here's how to clean it. Money laundering | https://amzn.to/3c6zRMu |
| T2 | The Square | Weapons of Mass Destruction – don't let them get on your nerves. A viral nerve agent being shipped by terrorists and WMDs | https://amzn.to/3sEiKYx |
| T3 | The Circle | The desert is no place to get lost. In the Arizona deserts, with the Navajo; about missiles stolen from storage. | https://amzn.to/3qLavYZ |
| T4 | Cosy | Cosy Crime in Devon | This novel |
| **Archangel Collection** | | | |
| A1 | Archangel | Sometimes I am necessary. Icelandic-born, Russian trained agent Christina Nott, learns her craft. | https://amzn.to/2Y9nB5K |
| A2 | Raven | An eye that sees all between darkness and light. Big business gone bad and being a freemason won't absolve you. | https://amzn.to/2MiGVe6 |
| A3 | Card Game | The power of Tarot whilst throwing oil on a troubled market | https://amzn.to/2Y8HLgs |
| A5 | Play On, Christina Nott | Money, Mayhem, Manipulation. Christina Nott, on Tour for the FSB | https://amzn.to/2MbkuHI |
| A6 | Corrupt | Parliamentary corruption. Trouble at the House | https://amzn.to/2M0HnOw |
| A7 | Sleaze | Autos, Politics, Gstaad | https://amzn.to/3sE3UDt |
| **Big Science** | | | |
| B1 | Coin | Get rich quick with Cybercash – just don't tell GCHQ | https://amzn.to/3o82wmS |
| B2 | An Unstable System | Creating the right kind of mind | https://amzn.to/2PRJciF |
| B3 | The Watcher | We don't need no personal saviours here. From the Big Bang to the almighty Whimper | https://amzn.to/3kTFWjg |
| B4 | Jump | Some kind of future. | https://amzn.to/3sCzK3h |

| | | | |
|---|---|---|---|
| B5 | Pulse | Sci-Fi dystopian blood management with nano-bots. Want more? Just stay away from the edge | https://amzn.to/3qQlBvL |
| B6 | Rage | A madman's war | https://amzn.to/3MEuKlL |

**Blade's Edge Trilogy**

| | | | |
|---|---|---|---|
| E1 | Edge | World end climate collapse and sham discovered during magnetite mining from Jupiter's moon Ganymede. | https://amzn.to/2KDmYOW |
| E2 | Edge Blue | Endgame, for Earth – unless? | https://amzn.to/2Kyq9au |
| E3 | Edge Red | Museum Earth an artificially intelligent outcome – unless? | https://amzn.to/2KzJwjz |

**Master Collections**

| | | | |
|---|---|---|---|
| C1/T4 | The Ox Stunner | The Triangle Trilogy – thick enough to stun an ox Triangle, Circle, Square in one heavy book. all feature Jake, Bigsy, Clare, Chuck Manners | https://amzn.to/3sHxlgh |
| C2/A4 | Magazine Clip | First three Archangel novels | https://amzn.to/3pbBJYn |
| C3/A8 | Ignoble | Corrupt and Sleaze omnibus – double album | https://amzn.to/3sp6EUL |
| C4/B7 | The Dealer | Jump, Pulse and Rage Collection | https://amzn.to/3AlZmWg |
| C5/E4 | Edge of Forever | Edge Trilogy | https://amzn.to/3c57Ghj |

# Rule 4: Consider everything an experiment

CONTENTS

**Thanks** **3**

**Author's Note** **4**

**Ed Adams Novels** **5**

PART ONE 12

**Preface** **13**
September Party 15

**To whoever stole the speedboat** **21**
Replacement Bus Services 22
Magser Deesum 26
Sleek black halter neck 32
Spotlight or searchlight? 35
Gilt-head bream 42

**Own it** **46**
Kegger 47
Careless accidental backhanders 54
Skateboards and Top Hats 59
Miel Doux Artists 73
Less than pristine turn out of the housemaid 76

**10 pm** **80**
Munch 81
Digestif 89
Lead pipe and rope 92
Into the Pygtle 96
Hot bodies 100

**There will be consequences** **106**
Solanaceae 107

Raggedy Groups 115

PART TWO 119

**I am the one who knocks** **121**
Fog of war 122
Joint State Threats Assessment Team 124
Flip 131
Autonomous vehicles 138
Trail of evidence 142

**I'm reviewing the situation** **149**
Wannabee 150
Pursuivants 154
Rigid Inflatable 159
Channelling Coachella 163
An instinctive form of theatre 169
Small insect on jacket 172
Don't cross the streams 182
Pace 183
M24 186
Sightseeing? 196
Open the briefcase 200
US PENTAGON - EYES ONLY 201
What we've just read 203
Emmanuelle's note 208
What they do in the shadows 209
Things we know 215
Bored stay-at-home parents 227

**A policeman's lot** **232**
Class A Problem 233
Camouflage 237

PART THREE 243

**Emmanuelle** **245**
Close-fitting 247
En Vogue 253
Apache AH64E 255
Scorpion Tail 263
Across the River 264
Kovarin 270

**Aurora** **273**
Side bar and extreme force 274
Negotiate 278
Sonic boom 287
London 290

# PART ONE

## *Preface*

I should explain: Clare Crafts and myself, Jake Lambers, were two of the three founders of our small investigation company called 'The Triangle'.

Together with Dave 'Bigsy' Carter we had formed the company after a particular adventure with multiple offshore interests. It had left us with an embarrassing amount of non-traceable money. More than enough to start our firm.

Then Clare's friend Christina had joined our tight-knit group. Christina's rather mixed background - Icelandic, with much time also spent in Russia, and her specialist knowledge of espionage meant that she became a natural fit in our little group.

From our very first adventure together, we'd met members of both the UK's and US Secret Service and were now occasionally commissioned off-book to run special investigations for them.

It had led to us establishing proper office premises in London - in Hay's Galleria, which was close to London Bridge and the River Thames and a short walk back into the City of London.

As a direct consequence of our original exploits, we had also befriended an American ex-marine named Chuck Manners, who seemed to move in circles somewhat similar to those of Christina.

Oh, and I should mention that Chuck was living with Amanda Miller, who was someone high-up the British Secret Service. Despite my journalism background, the Chuck and Amanda revelation was a complete surprise to me.

Clare and I have a complicated past relationship with Amanda and helped her with certain situations.

## *September Party*

I had joked about a wild party.

But this was something else. We were invited to the celebration of Emmanuelle Catteau and Jago Fox's engagement and told that there would be some intriguing guests present. It was down on the south-west coast of England, in Devon, a few miles from the city of Exeter.

What could possibly go wrong with a celebration at a large house looking out over the River Exe?

It starts when Clare calls my cellphone.

"Fancy a party?" she asks, "We've been emailed by Emmanuelle Catteau. I think she's about to get engaged to Jago Fox."

I remembered Emmanuelle (then) Barbet from Cambridge. She was a hot friend of Clare. It was great to be in her crowd, but otherwise, she would be relatively unapproachable. She gained the inevitable nickname of Barbie.

Then there was Jago - the consummate playboy. He and I used to go together to some of the parties. The first time I met him, we were on a speedboat borrowed from his girlfriend, except she didn't know anything about it. It created a great deal of short-term trouble.

Jago was lightly studying economics, and I was hard at work with English. Jago often said he'd picked the wrong university. They made us work at Cambridge, with weekly papers and problems. Jago had the impression that it was easier, in certain subjects, to 'get by' at Oxford. He cited the resultant politicians produced as examples.

Emmanuelle and Jago had been friends ever since I can remember, and although there was talk of a torrid relationship between the two of them, I had it parked with other gossip.

"How come you've been invited?" I asked.

"It's WE, actually. Jago remembered you were something to do with journalism and wanted you to do a car-themed article, whilst you are with him."

"Typical Jago. But don't you think it's presumptuous

to link us together?"

"No, it's been sent to our business address - The Triangle - in Hays Galleria. Although I must admit my name comes first!"

I thought back to my time before we'd started The Triangle. I'd worked for a magazine called Street, back in the days when lifestyle magazines were still a thing. Before social media shooed most of them from the racks in WH Smith.

"But Jago must know I don't write now?" I ask.

"It's surprising how much he and Emmanuelle seem to know about both of us," answered Clare.

"How embarrassing that I've not really thought about either of them since we left Cambridge."

"Well, there's something I didn't know, which makes more sense of everything now," answered Clare, "I never knew they were close neighbours down in Devon - near Exeter!"

"I went with Jago once to his father's pile down that way - 'Massive Mansion' or something it was called. It was very picturesque. Looked out onto the River Exe. They had butlers and staff. I think they turned part of it over to visiting businesspeople as a kind of up-scale hotel. To help it pay its way - it even had a massive helipad. I seem to remember that even back then it was £30k and up per week."

"A kind of high-end Airbnb? - Well, almost next door to it is now Emmanuelle's place - they are probably in the same postcode. Emmanuelle married but then became a widow. Her husband, Hans Catteau, bought the place and lived there until his untimely death. It was a combination of booze and drugs, apparently."

"How are you so well informed?" I ask, "And by the way, if you'd seen Jago's family place, you wouldn't say that about postcodes. His home was so large it must have its own postcode. Postcodes, if you were to include the vineyard."

Clare answers, "I keep up with the social media. And I still swap emails with Emmanuelle. I remember when she lost Hans. She was distraught. But she did inherit his recently acquired home - Seymour House - it sounds far more modest that Jago's place but is still a proper mansion."

"What do all those people in Devon do?" I ask.

"They used to make ships, but nowadays they grow apples, make cider and farm. That and have tidy incomes from their previous companies, pensions, and investments!"

I decided Clare was now being facetious, although I had a sneaking feeling that she could be right.

"So, what are they both doing?" I ask.

Clare replies, "Emmanuelle Catteau is nowadays a well-known socialite and Jago Fox pretends to be a Lord of the Manor."

"No surprise with Emmanuelle - I assume she will have a few pop stars and celebs at the party?" I enquire hopefully.

"Yes, she says it will be 'A-List'. Jago is inviting some of his business clients. I suspect that is why he wants you along - to talk about cars."

"Why? What's his business now?" I ask.

"Inherited from his father, it's called FST, and makes the Ikiru chipset for motor vehicles. They are in incredible demand nowadays because more cars are becoming electric."

"FST? That's a big name in the motor world. And I seem to remember that Ikiru are Artificial Intelligence chips. But that's all I know."

Clare answers, "My knowledge is more prosaic. His father started in the '70s and first built circuits for radios but then transitioned to car innards. I guess

Jago must have inherited the company when his father passed away around four years ago."

I smile, "You mention that Jago will act like a Lord of the Manor. Yes, that's him exactly. One amusing thing I remember was that from his house you could see out across the River to the other side - maybe a mile away. On it was a castle and it, in turn, was owned by a real Lord. Not only that, but the real Lord also didn't have the airs and graces that Jago tried so hard to emulate - It's like Jago has swallowed the Downton Abbey playbook."

"Oh, we've just got to say yes," giggles Clare.

What could possibly go wrong?

## *To whoever stole the speedboat*

To whoever stole the speedboat
I want you to know that you ruined Easter

I know some facts.
You listen to classical music,
you like orange things,
you have a wonder cabinet of bird wings and found objects.
One of these is a pair of swimming goggles you found on the
tarmac of terminal 3 on your way back from Jordan.

You know, given the chance, I would trade
information about you to the government for a year's
supply of tinned orange segments.

But since I think you might be a killer,
and all the evidence I have collated
is unsubstantiated, you can keep the water machine.

I am going to become a kite specialist.
Look out for coloured strings.

*Hannah Walker*

*Replacement Bus Services*

We took the streamlined express from Paddington to Exeter. In a couple of hours, we were in a green and pleasant landscape, having seen glimpses of the sea, before running along parallel with the main Devon and Cornwall motorway.

Then a rainy Exeter. It amused us both that outside the station on a prominent 'Exeter' sign was permanent signage for rail replacement buses. A man with an umbrella was holding a sign with "Lambers and Craft" on it, which we took to be ours. He shows us to a sleek, modern electric car and assists place our luggage in the back. I notice it looks more like a limo service than a regular taxi and we take our seats in the back for the cosseted journey to Magister Grange.

Out of the central area, the buildings soon gave way to glimpses of the river and rain-swept fields. I could remember nothing of my prior journey to

Jago's place, except that the area had an unusual pronunciation.

I ask the taxi driver, who replies, 'I'm originally from north London, but I think the correct way to say 'Magister Grange, Dittlesham' is ' Magser Deesum'. There are quite a few unusual pronunciations around here."

"Well, that's handy," crows Clare, "Now we have some useful local knowledge."

"Even if it comes from Highbury," replies the taxi driver, "Say, are you here for the event at the rugby ground? Something to do with cars? I can give you my direct number if you like?"

"No, that's fine," says Clare, "I'll take your card, but we won't be going to the rugby ground."

I couldn't help wondering if there was some kind of angle on this whole event. Something with the fingerprints of Jago all over it.

Then the drive into Magister Grange. It reminds me of something from another era, perhaps Brideshead with a long drive across well-manicured fields. Then through a gate and an inner walled area which leads, via another drive to the main house. I remember the half-moon shaped approach into the property. The taxi swings around and pulls up outside the main door. Almost immediately, it opens, and a man dressed as a butler greets us. I notice the rain has gone and we have bright sunshine.

"Mr. Fox will be along to greet you shortly; he is showing other guests to their room."

We climb from the car, and the driver opens the boot.

"No, Sir, Madam, You won't need to carry your bags. I'll see that they get to your rooms."

I notice his use of plural and the butler smiles. "Mr. Fox asked that you be given adjoining rooms, in any case."

I try to remember how many rooms there were at the Grange but can't. It was at least twenty bedrooms, plus a whole servants' quarter for the staff. Think of a small hotel, rather than a private dwelling.

The butler shows us into a huge reception room, maybe 15 metres long and 8 metres wide. I recognise it as somewhere from my previous visit, and almost unchanged. There is a floor of black-and-white marble squares, set on the diagonal, a large fireplace on the long wall, and three sets of sofas set up so that a large gathering could conveniently talk to one another. The ceiling is dramatically painted blue with small yellow stars and a majestic sunburst in the middle.

"Masonic," whispers Clare. I nod in agreement.

"Adapted masonic," I add.

We look at one another. This could be an interesting couple of days.

*Magser Deesum*

Now we are in an entrance lobby, looking at the stairs, when we hear the approaching footsteps and then in strides Jago Fox.

"My dears," he says, looking toward us both, with outstretched arms, "Welcome to Deesum!"

"Oh yes, we heard about Magser Deesum," answers Clare, and we all laugh.

Jago wears a hounds tooth check three-piece suit. It seems to be mainly brown with a faint lime background and a sky blue large square check. I haven't described it very well, but it looked country chic. White cotton poplin shirt and a navy-blue twill tie. Last button of waistcoat undone. The very model of a country squire. A cross between dashing and something from central casting. It made our metro casual black and white attire seem very drab, yet it would be almost impossible to wear his outfit in our part of London.

He walks to Clare, hugs her, and then to me. I receive the same hug and notice the expensive cologne he was wearing. I still detect in his mannerisms something 'off' about him, like he is trying hard to conceal something.

"It is so good to see you both!" he exclaims, "There will be so much to talk about, and I'll want to introduce you to a few of my high-octane friends."

"But is this really about getting engaged?" asks Clare, "If so, then 'Congratulations!'"

"Yes, it really is. The main event is tomorrow evening." Jago answers, "Can you believe it? That Emmanuelle and I were once a much gossiped about 'item' in Cambridge and now, after becoming neighbours, we are ready to tie the knot!"

"But I hear Emmanuelle had a rough time of it?" asks Clare.

"We shouldn't speak ill of those not with us, but let's say her husband, Hans, was an addict. Booze and cocaine. Along the way, he used to run into rages, and Emmanuelle bore the brunt of a few of them. He died of an O.D."

"Overdose?" asks Clare.

"Yes, there was a post-mortem and everything was dragged through courtrooms. They hadn't been married long and so it attracted all kinds of unpleasant gossip about their relationship and Emmanuel's motives against him. No case to answer, of course."

I looked across to Clare and realise she didn't seem to know this.

Jago continues, "And there's a similar story for me, I'm afraid. After Cambridge, I fell head over heels in love with Katie. That's Katie Law. I'd been visiting her whilst I was finishing my studies. She helped me to recoup some of my squandered time and she was technically my tutor. She was older than me by some eight years and I suppose I was seduced by her experience."

"Here's to you, Mrs Robinson?" asked Clare.

"Kind of like that. We used to meet at her rooms which were very central. You know the Corpus Clock? By the Chop House. Well, she had rooms just along from there. First floor, Little more than a bedsit, well, except there was a separate study room. She had a range of ne'er-do-wells come to visit her and gave private tuition. The atmosphere between us was surprisingly electric and then, one day, she answered her door in a bathrobe."

I see Clare smile. I realise this was not an unusual situation for Jago. I presume Clare was thinking the same.

"Well, one thing led to another, and I found the need to step up my sessions with Katie. By the time I left Cambridge, I was already engaged and after another six months we were married."

"How is it we didn't hear about any of this?" I ask.

"To be honest, I thought if I told friends, someone might try to talk me out of it. I mean, how does it look? Rich landowning lad speared by penniless tutor."

"What happened?" I ask, "I mean, you are not married now. How did you split up?"

"Very similar to Emmanuelle's situation, actually. Katie was a dipso. I didn't realise how much she drank until it was too late."

Clare and I both noticed Jago's use of dipso - dipsomaniac - which was now a seldom used term. I decided he was trying to isolate himself from thinking about alcohol use disorder.

Jago continued as if he'd had to tell this story many times.

"Katie had been binge drinking alone when it happened. Her BAC - blood alcohol content was over 1. Much higher than the 0.4 which is usually regarded as a guide-level maximum and it was the equivalent of around 20 hurriedly consumed drinks. That is more than a complete bottle of vodka. They say her body went into shutdown."

A pause. Clare and I didn't know what to say.

Jago starts again, "But I didn't want to load you with such sombre tales, but it's better you hear it from me than try to piece it together from the gossip around the party. Look, I'm over it now and am thrilled at the prospect of moving forward together with Emmanuelle."

"Were there any children?" asked Clare.

"One...Christopher," answered Jago, "He was Katie's son from her previous marriage. She had him when she was just sixteen and when we got married, he was already eighteen years old. His name is Christopher Law. After an initial period of instability, he eventually became like my own son, and therefore somewhat wayward. I'm afraid to say he has something of a bad reputation in Dittlesham. He's twenty-four now. I expect you will see him tomorrow."

I was feeling overloaded. I guess if I'd had to tell Jago of our haphazard lifestyle it would sound just as crazy, but I could see how the local gossips of Dittlesham could piece this together. Everybody noticed that Jago Fox and Mrs. Emmanuelle Catteau got on very well together. After her husband's death, the intimacy became more marked. They were always seen about together, and it was freely conjectured that at the end of a suitable period of mourning, Mrs. Catteau would become Mrs. Jago Fox.

There was a certain symmetry about the situation. Jago Fox's wife Katie had died of drink. Hans Catteau had been a drunkard for years before his death. It was only fitting that these two victims of alcoholic excess should make up to each other for all that they had previously endured at the hands of their former spouses.

*Sleek black halter neck*

The butler reappears and then Emmanuelle appears in the doorway. She looks fantastic. Like a sex goddess film star in a sleek black halter neck. 'Blue-eyed boy bait' as we used to say. Now, the phrase needs an upgrade. No country girl looks for Emmanuelle next to Jago. I worry that I've just made a sharp, noisy intake of breath.

Before I can say anything, Emmanuelle strides over and plants a luscious kiss on my mouth.

"Jago! How could you keep it from me that Jake and Clare have arrived?" She spins and clutches Clare in a warm embrace. I can see that Emmanuelle has hardly changed. She is just like she was at Cambridge, only perhaps even more glamorous.

"My god, Emmanuelle, you look as gorgeous as ever!" I utter, with Clare nodding her approval.

"Thank you, but I'm just so excited to see you both! You both look the same, no! better! than you did at Cambridge. Delightful. I heard you work together too, but nothing more than platonic?" She looks at Clare.

"You, Mademoiselle, are as cheeky as ever!" laughs Clare, "Look, where do you keep the drinks? We must sit down together and bring each other up-to-date."

I can sense the years fall away as we all revert to Cambridge-style relations with one-another.

Emmanuelle continues, "Yes, I've a few other guests to greet this evening, but I think I'll be able to sneak away, especially if Jago stays on duty along with Pascal Duret our butler!"

Jago nods acquiescence, "Go on you two. I've Jake here to help me be the 'meeter greeter'. We'll also be able to reacquaint properly. And - trade secret - we suggested we'd meet the trains and planes into Exeter with cars, so we know when most people will arrive!"

"What about those driving?"

"At a normal speed, it takes most people almost two minutes to get from the main gate to outside the front door! That's enough time for us to deploy a champagne greeting!"

*Spotlight or searchlight?*

I stay with Jago, and we chat about the past and our recent fortunes. He avoids talking further about his first wife, Katie, and also stays away from talking about Emmanuelle. I sense he has another secret pulling him down, but he remains tight-lipped about whatever it is.

He says to me, "Look Jake, there's some business going down here this weekend and I'm afraid they have rather put me under the spotlight. It has kind of changed to a searchlight though, and I'm the one being sought. Don't believe what you hear about me over the weekend."

I ask him to elaborate.

He changes the subject. "You know, I've linked our engagement party on to an event which is being held in Exeter. Kill two birds, one might say."

'Cashing-in,' I thought. This was Jago all over. An event which he could take advantage of. A way to throw a lavish party event without paying for everything. Same old Jago.

"Yes, I've agreed to take some of the VIPs attending the special event at the rugby stadium in Exeter. It's about car technology - especially batteries - and there are a few special guests who don't want to stay at the usual hotels. I've got a helipad here so we can ferry people to the event in ten minutes. Everyone wins. They get fine wine and dine here; luxury accommodation yet can still get to their meetings in Exeter. And they can discuss more sensitive business here, instead of in the noisy ambience of the main event."

Then Jago switches subjects. I could tell he wanted to keep things 'light' and he diverts to talking about a strange encounter he'd had at Uni.

"I don't think I ever told you about my first term at Uni. It was before we met. It was partway through Michaelmas and I had been set a Philosophy essay topic. I'll never forget. It was about contrasting Bertrand Russell's 1905 paper 'On Denoting' and Peter Strawson's 1950 article 'On Referring'. I think I called it 'The battle of the quantifiers' ."

"That's a lot to remember!" I say, "And to argue." I was intrigued why he'd remembered this moment in time.

"Well, my tutor listened to my incredibly naïve explanation of what I thought Strawson meant, and carefully tried to explain why I'd got it wrong. I argued back and thought I was holding my ground. After a while, she went out of the office, and knocked softly on the open door opposite. A very old, kindly looking man looked up from his desk.

" 'Professor Strawson, would you mind explaining to this student why he is wrong?'

"Yes, Strawson had been sitting listening to the whole encounter!"

"I'd forgotten that these universities have experts on tap. To be honest, I look back on it as a defining moment. The moment when I decided I'd better get a personal tutor to help me."

Now I could see why he remembers it. The trigger event that led to him enrolling with Katie and their subsequent relationship.

"Yes, sometimes we don't realise the small decisions we make that affect the rest of our lives." He looked wistful for a moment and then, as if a spell was broken, he grinned and looked toward the door.

"Zdrastvui!" he utters and then heartily shakes the

hand of a handsome, tanned, tall man who had entered the room accompanied by an exotic wrap-around woman. She separated from him with the movement of a gentle cat.

Jago and the man shake hands and then embrace in a manly-back-slapping way.

"Hello, my friend - This is Adam - Moskvin Adam Antonovich to give him his full name, and this is my dear friend from Cambridge, Jake Lambers. And who, Adam, is this delightful lady?"

"Hello," deep voiced, she gently extends an arm and hand, which Jago respectfully kisses, "My name is Shmagina Alina Petrovna - call me Alina. I'm, like Adam, also from Russia, a place close to Sankt Petersburg." She is in a pretty black silk dress, with leather lace-up boots which run half-way up her legs.

I mutter something about being delighted to meet her, all the while thinking that Jago's place is getting crowded with beautiful women.

Adam smiles, "Ah, it will be good to meet someone to back up Jago's stories that he studied at Cambridge. I'm pleased to meet you, Jake, but wonder why I'm already inside the hall? What's this? No reception outside!" Hardly any hint of accent.

Jago laughs, "No, we were engrossed in old student stories. I must have missed the two-minute-warning from Pascal, my butler!"

"Excuses, excuses," laughs Adam. I could see that Jago and Adam share affection for one another, although I also had the impression that Alina was a recent addition to Adam's friendship circle.

Then, more commotion as a small group enters the room, escorted by the butler.

Jago smiles, "Ah, Amelia, you seem to have found several of our guests! We can all get introduced now!"

I looked towards a slender woman, slim hipped, wiry, and almost boyish. I decide she must run a lot of triathlons to exhibit such signs of fitness.

"Amelia Brophy is our party co-ordinator. If you need anything, please just ask Amelia and I'm sure she will figure it out for you."

Amelia smiles, "Yes, and here we have Bettina Kübler, a Swiss researcher from Brant in Geneva. And in order for you boys to talk about cars, here's Hubert Tempelmann, the European Chief Technology Officer of the Zillian electric car company.

"And if cars are not your thing, then here's the one and only Drax - Alex Haynes, rapper star and someone of whom Emmanuelle is a great fan! And that is not all! We also have - all the way from Canada - Josh Harper from the band Erebus. They've just completed a world tour, including Russia, Japan, and the USA. And we should not forget Ian Salterton, a local book author who writes commandingly about this local area around Devon."

As each were introduced, they wave and smile. I notice that another attractive blonde wasn't introduced by Amelia and also note that she appears to be with Bettina. Drax and Joshua Harper both do a giant festival bow, and I realised it was something instinctive from their times on the road. I could see that Josh was with someone unannounced, but Drax appeared to be unaccompanied. I surmised that there could be too much gossip for his image.

I could also see a small huddle of 'extras' in the background and assumed that at least some guests had brought support staff. My guess was that Tempelmann would have an assistant, Haynes/Drax, a stylist, PR person, maybe some backup singers. Harper, I decided, would have a girlfriend, although I assumed that the local author would be alone.

"We're going to need more champagne!" says Jago

and gestures to Amelia Brophy. Almost instantly a couple of servers wheel in a large trolley of glasses, ice buckets, and bottles of Bollinger.

This party was starting a whole day early. Typical Jago.

## *Gilt-head bream*

It is 6pm.

"You'll all be joining us for dinner this evening?" asks Jago.

I look at Clare. We hadn't eaten since the railway food at Paddington.

"Of course," we both answer.

"I have a feeling we'll have a cast of thousands tonight," answers Jago, "Seven for seven thirty seem alright?"

"Delightful," answers Clare.

We go to our rooms and Jago has given us both a prime view across the lawns and to the river.

"I expect Emmanuelle had something to do with this," says Clare as we look around, "To give us such lovely accommodation."

I flick on the television, start the electric kettle, and we both flop onto my bed to watch a late afternoon quiz show accompanied by coffee and shortbread biscuits.

At about 6:30pm there is a quiet tap on the door. I get up to answer it, pondering the quiz question of the name of the fictional suburb in which 'The Bill' TV series had been set. Was it Walford?

At the door is Amelia Brophy. The party organiser.

"Hello," she says, "I tapped lightly in case you were sleeping. The dinner is in around a half hour and I was checking among the guests for any undeclared allergies. You know the kind of things - nuts, wheat, milk, shellfish..." I believe the first course from Cook tonight will be scallops, maybe with some eel. All locally sourced of course."

I open the door wider so that Amelia can see Clare standing by the window.

"No, we're both fine. Anything goes, as they say."

"Okay, well, let me leave you the menu. There aren't officially any alternative choices, but if Cook knows in advance, then she says she will rustle up something. Oh, and I should say that the dining this evening is informal. No need to dress up."

She smiles.

"That's very thoughtful," I say, "Thank you."

Clare speaks, "That woman; she reminds me of someone, you know, but I can't quite place it."

I finger the substantially thick card that the menu is printed upon, "Let's look at this menu...I imagine Jago won't disappoint."

***Starters:*** *Lyme Bay scallop ceviche, avocado, Exmoor caviar, citrus vinaigrette*
*2015 Pebblebed Vineyard, Madeleine Angevine, Phoenix and Seyval Blanc.*

***Fish:*** *Local barbecued Gilt-head bream, St Enodoc asparagus, preserved lemon, parsley cream*
*2016 Château Bouscassé, Pacherenc du Vic-Bilh Sec, France*

***Entree:*** *Locally sourced lamb, Devon vegetables, courgette and basil, lamb tapenade jus*
*2018 Vacqueyras 'Cuvée des Templiers', Domaine Le Clos des Cazaux, Rhône*

***Pudding:*** *Dart's apples tarte Tatin, Calvados caramel &*

*smoked milk ice cream*
*2011 Tokaji Late Harvest, Tokaj, Hungary*

"He's really caught the Devon bug!" exclaims Clare, "Look at it. Even the first wine is from Devon."

"But St Enodoc is in Cornwall. It's near to Padstow."

"Well, the apples are local, but I think this part of Devon is more known for cider apples," answers Clare.

"He's pushing the boat out with this though, I guess he wants to impress!"

"As if the whole of Magister Grange isn't enough!"

We look at one another and decide it is time to prepare to go downstairs for the meal.

## *Own it*

*Lighters up, lighters up*
*One time, lighters up*
*Pulled up in the party*
*When you saw me I was lighting up my J*
*So go ahead and brighten up my day*
*Lighters in the air when you're lighting up the rave*

*Jonathan Lee / Edward Christopher Sheeran / Damini Ebunoluwa Ogulu / Michael Ebenazer Kwadjo Omari Owuo Junior / Fred*

## *Kegger*

As we walked into the Dining Room I caught an immediate sense of Jago up to usual tricks. There were spaces for a dozen around the main table although most were standing up chatting to one another.

A second table appeared to be for the remaining guests, who I determined were mainly local folk from around the area. I'd assumed we'd be on the second table, but no, we'd been placed amid the main group.

I could see Jago chatting to Adam Antonovich, who Clare had already googled and was a Russian from a money house. Together in a group were Bettina Kübler - a Swiss researcher at Brant, Geneva, working on eDefence and Hubert Tempelmann, the CTO for Zillian car company, earnestly talking about electric cars. Clare didn't like to be caught out and had been hitting Google.

Ian Salterton, the local book author, was already seated, talking earnestly talking to Joshua Harper about shipbuilding along the River Exe. Apparently Josh's band was named after a ship built in a local shipyard. Next to Josh sat his girlfriend, who Clare instantly recognises.

"Jallie? It's Clare! And hey Josh - what on earth are you doing here?"

"Clare Crafts! Put it here!" says Josh, standing and wrapping both his arms around Clare. Jallie T jumps up too, gives a squee of delight, then hugs Clare and kisses her on both cheeks.

Clare turns toward me. "Remember that time Christina and I took off a road trip with a band? It was Jallie T's band and Christina was supporting Erebus on tour!"

I remembered it well, but had never met Jallie T or Josh.

"Incredible! So how do you know Emmanuelle and Jago?" I ask, trying to piece things together.

"Well, you remember that Emmanuelle was originally from Canada - Emmanuelle Barbet? - She was from Vancouver, which is the self-same town that I'm from," explained Josh. We both went to the same school - Byng Arts in West Point, Vancouver. I was studying music and Emmanuelle was, in those days, a fine arts student. I used to go with some friends and we'd jam open air on acoustic guitars around Jericho Beach. Emmanuelle and some of her girl friends used to come visit sometimes. It was very convenient for all of us. I even wrote a song about Emmanuelle, but our band never played it. Come to think of it, it was in French."

He looked around, wrapped in his thoughts, and then blurted, "Of course it would be entirely inappropriate to sing it here - with the engagement party tomorrow and all!"

"But you're not a thing with Jallie now?" asks Clare.

Josh and Jallie both laugh, "No - keep up, Clare. We've just finished a tour of Italy, Germany and France and should be on our way back to Canada. Then Josh got the call from Emmanuelle and needed a plus one!"

"Hold on then, what about Rishi? You were an item back then?"

Jallie laughs, "Still are. Rishi's outside helping the rig-out for the gig tomorrow. Compared with Stadiums, this is back pocket stuff, but it made it easy for him to accompany me to this kegger."

"I don't think Jago would like to hear it being called a kegger," says Clare, "Have you seen the wine list? And that's just for tonight."

"You know something," says Jallie, "You get to sense when there's too much money around. Like when we played the South of France or Miami. Then it's time to listen out for the strange accents. Well, not including Canadian, of course!"

She looks at me.

"This attractive man? I'm guessing he is with you?"

"Hello," I say, "I'm Jake - I've heard such a lot about you and that big road trip from Clare and Christina. Both Erebus and Jallie T's part. Something I remember about illuminated mallets?"

"Oh, don't get me started," jokes Josh, "Those damn mallets. I think Rishi was trying to get rid of them, but they became an integral part of Jallie's warm-up act. Some might say scene stealing!"

At that moment, Drax appears and joins the group. "Hi, I'm Alec Haynes - Drax - I could hear you talking about music, I've been asked to perform here tomorrow evening."

Josh and Drax shake hands in an amusingly formal way.

Clare and Josh seemed to know all about Drax, who I now realise comes from south London and was a well-known black grime artist.

"I get confused about the difference between hip-hop, garage and grime..." I begin.

"Ha, you won't be the first," smiles Drax. "Grime is electronic music that emerged in London in the early 2000s. It developed from UK garage, jungle, dancehall, and hip hop. We use rapid, syncopated breakbeats, at around 140 beats per minute, with aggressive jagged electronic sounds. Emceeing is a significant element of the style, with our lyrics about urban life."

Wow. I asked for that. The description sounded to me like performance computer programming.

Josh cuts in, "Think of Dizzee Rascal, Kano, Rizzle Kicks, and Wiley. And, of course, Stormzy. It's also big in Canada, although the genre has been described as the 'most significant musical development within the UK for decades.' "

Jallie speaks, "Yes, Drax, I've heard your sounds. I liked 'Lost' and 'Skip' a lot. I'm Jallie T - here without my small band from Canada."

"Great to meet you all. Josh, you're a muso too?"

"Yeah, lead guitar with Erebus, we've just been on a Euro-tour,"

"Amazing that we are all here for this mini-fest. The car industry has too much money to splash. Do any of you already know Emmanuelle Catteau and Jago Fox - I'm told they are getting engaged?"

We all nod. "... Only I was asked to do the gig for the car show - or whatever it is - by the party organiser - Amelia Brophy. She says that Emmanuelle is a fan, although I've not said 'hello' yet."

"We'll soon fix that," says Clare, who makes an immediate beeline for Emmanuelle - literally pulling her by the hand back across the room.

"Here we are, Emmanuelle - meet Drax - Alex Haynes!"

"Oh. My. God. I've listened to everything you've made. Even those offcuts - what were they called 'Inner'? I'll have to get some pictures of us together! Clare, help me out here!"

Clare points her iPhone at the two of them and takes around half a dozen pictures. Drax and Emmanuelle are wrapped around one another by the third photograph.

"Easy, Cougar!" says Clare, "Save some for the rest of us." We all laugh, just as a gong sounds.

Amelia announces, "Dinner is served," and we all hunt for our place settings around the table.

## *Careless accidental backhanders*

7:30 pm

I'm seated near to one end of the table. It's close to Jago, but away from the musicians. Clare is right at the other end, with Jallie, Josh and Alec. Emmanuelle is also at the far end of the table.

I meet two new faces. Lawrence Booth, an ex-MP who used to live in the area and is returning. I think he left Parliament under a cloud. Nothing too spectacular, but something involving taking some careless accidental backhanders. He is with Bianca Hart, a foxy lady that doesn't seem to quite fit with Lawrence's persona. Bianca is to my right, and Lawrence has been placed opposite her. Next to Bianca is the author whose name I can't remember. Someone just called him Ian.

To my left is Bettina Kübler the Swiss researcher from Brant, who is working on eDefence. Next to her, at the head of the table sits Jago. Then, opposite Bettina is Hubert Tempelmann, the CTO for Zillian, the car company. Opposite me is Adam Antonovich, the monied Russian.

I can see what is happening. Jago is using this session to further some business aim. He has obviously told Emmanuelle what he is doing, and she has drawn the non-players in Jago's plan to the other end of the table. Next to Adam sits Stéphane Gérard, the close friend of Bettina.

Jago has bookended the business-concentrated part of the table with two beautiful women, Stéphane, and Bianca. Then the table morphs towards the show-business arts and cultural end, crowned with Emmanuelle.

It's a clever move, and something I'd always expect Jago to do. After a bit of small talk about the Exeter Chiefs rugby team and yachts, we move on to the more business-like subject of automobiles and the whacky trade show in Exeter, which seems to be mainly about batteries. I gather from the conversation that Lawrence Booth has set up some kind of motoring lobby organisation since he left Parliament. I can see why Jago plonked me into this group, although I can't help feeling that the group at the Emmanuelle end of the table is going to have more fun and banter.

Lawrence's partner for the evening, Bianca Hart, looks attentive enough, but I can sense that she has realised that there are more powerful people around the table than Lawrence Booth. At one point, Adam Antonovich asks Bianca if she would like water and she replies 'Da'. I engage her in small talk about the beauties of Devon and how confusing it is that there is a Lord Devon, but still ordinary people could have Devon as a surname. I say my acquaintance Jennifer Sussex is a case in point. I can see her react as I mention this name. She purses her lips and shakes her head as if to say, 'now is not the time'.

I realise I've just identified her as another of Jennifer's legion of escorts to the great and the good, supplied via Miel Doux Artists, an outfit we had a run-in with, in London some time ago.

Next to Bianca, the local author - whose name I picked up as Ian Salterton - is looking overwhelmed by the prospect of sitting near to the glamorous Bianca, who I can see is very capable of softly Cosying up to whoever is nearby. I decide to bring Salterton into the conversation, so I ask him some things about the local area.

He looks thankful to have some male conversation and talks across Bianca. "Our village, Dittlesham, is very much like any other village with a neat row of pretty shops. Nowadays, I suggest that the main hobby is 'goss-sip.'" I sense Salterton is sloshed already. Unaccompanied and overwhelmed by the company, he has been tenaciously drinking.

I could see that Jago was completely immersed in car-talk with Bettina, Hubert, and Adam and so when Salterton lowered his voice to say the next thing, I was quite struck by his level of uninhibited directness and hoped that Jago had not heard.

"All the time that Katie's son - that's Christopher Law - was growing up to manhood a series of lady housekeepers presided over Fox's establishment, and each was regarded as a possible wife for Jago." Salterton's words were a little slurred and he was waving his glass of wine around somewhat demonstratively.

Salterton adds, "The last of them, a lithesome woman called Abigail Holbrook, has reigned undisputed for some time, longer than any of her predecessors. But for Emmanuelle, Jago Fox could hardly have escaped.

"That, and the unexpected arrival of Fox's widowed sister-in-law from Canada. Mrs. Cecilia Fox helped put Miss Holbrook in her proper place. The Foxes seemed an unlucky family."

Jago looked up from his car-talk when he heard Salterton mention Cecilia. I smiled back and said, "Oh Jago, Ian was just telling me you have your sister-in-law staying here now!"

Jago smiled, "Yes Cecilia and Emmanuelle get on like a house on fire!"

Jago grins and says to me, "But come on Jake, you must have an opinion about what we are discussing. You used to write all about cars for that magazine of yours!"

Thanks, Jago, nice set-up.

Hubert Tempelmann speaks, "The future of car design is all about skateboards and top hats. That's the flat, often self-supporting chassis of an electric vehicle, housing a large battery pack in the middle and motors at either end, along with the suspension, brakes and wheels."

I can see why this group wanted to be away from the main car convention visitors.

I say, "Almost like a slot car racer?" I think that Tempelmann is running a talk track from some kind of corporate presentation.

"Exactly. Upon the skateboard sits the top hat, which is car designer-speak for the body and interior of a vehicle."

Bettina Kübler interjects, "It's not so difficult to transfer similar thinking to an armoured vehicle." I realise Bettina is not with her apparent soul-mate Stéphane Gérard.

Hubert nods, "With far fewer moving parts than an internal combustion engine, the battery pack and motors in this skateboard chassis perform in a near-universal way, no matter which manufacturer the vehicle comes from."

Bettina persists, "Think also, instead of having to get diesel fuel to the position of the armoured vehicle. Instead, an electric armament can be plugged into any convenient power source and recharged over a period varying from 30 minutes to overnight."

Hubert agrees, "Yes. Think about it. In a tank, the power output can be changed, along with battery size and the voltage of the system architecture. Need a quick turnaround? Make the batteries exchangeable."

Bettina adds, "So a battlefront tank could be de-coupled from the vagaries of the logistical supply chain. Plug and play."

"Plug and destroy," I mutter and everyone looks across to me.

"You're missing the point, Jake," says Jago, "Imagine a whole new class of armaments. Nimble and powerful. With self-driving assistance and radio control, these units could even be deployed with no one inside."

"That's like an ultimate weapon."

Now it's Moskvin Adam Antonovich's turn, "With still some superiority based upon tracked vehicle, the electric tank opens up a new class of battlefield management."

Adam continues, "Like the now abandoned Future Offensive Air System, one has to view these things in the round. There were other technologies catching up with FOAS - the idea of UAVs - it originally stood for Unmanned Air Vehicles before it got a politically correct, but even more menacing name, 'Uninhabited Air Vehicles'.

"And there's a clear difference. Wars are still about conquering territory. Think of Ukraine. Fighting is still like something from the last century. Pieces on a chessboard. Owning the Square. Air superiority sounds fine, but it isn't enough."

I'm reminded of that ex-Royal making a statement about chess pieces before he got a fatwa ruling against himself.

"It's battlefield superiority," said Bettina, "And that's where Brant comes in. Security systems are ready for deployment. C3I becomes SC3I. Secure Command, Control, Communication, and Intelligence are needed after C3I has worked its course. C3I for Combat Operations and then SC3I for secure management of outcomes. My company, Brant, specialise in such matters."

I wondered what kind of conversation I'd dropped in on, and then the penny dropped. Jago's company - the one inherited from his father called FST - makes the Ikiru chipset for motor vehicles. Electric motor vehicles. Not only that - but they also use Artificial Intelligence.

Jago adds, "Really, this is a conversation for the rest of the week. Jake, I don't think I mentioned we are having a week discussing car battery strategies through to 2030?"

What a topic. What on earth will they find to talk about? But it is as I suspected. Jago is mixing his engagement party with a work function. We are here for his engagement, but it becomes clearer that after the engagement party, the rest of the week is filled with discussions with the automotive industry.

Typical Jago is 'holding court' with these industry luminaries. Not only pop stars, but I assume further celebrities and probably a minor royal or two will probably get added to the mix before the week is out.

Hubert adds, "In a not-so-distant future, car manufacturers like Zillian could buy these electric skateboard chassis from a third party, the way they make computers with similar components inside everybody's system.

Bettina continues, "Brant is positioning to be the 'Intel Inside' for EV. What we bring is a blank canvas... any shape of vehicle, any size, any weight, any kind of body technology and autonomy."

"Even armaments?" I ask.

"Explicitly armaments. It's part of Brant's heritage," Bettina answers.

I think warfare is a strange form of heritage.

At that moment, there is a noise from along the table. I look around to see that Ian Salterton is looking somewhat bedraggled. I sense Bianca has helped him empty his wine glass all over himself. He must have said something quite offensive, and

Lawrence Booth is now speaking sternly to Salterton.

"Look Mr Salterton; this is not the way to behave in polite company. I hope you will apologise to Bianca now for what you said and then I hope we can draw a line under it."

Salterton looks confused, "I'm sorry, Bianca, Lawrence, everyone, and I realise I've caused a scene. I'd better go freshen up."

Jago stands and looks along the table.

"This local wine is pretty strong, you know. Sometimes it can loosen a fellow's tongue a little too far."

Salterton stands unsteadily and then weaves his way to the door.

"Ms Brophy? Now we'll need another chap to fill Mr Salterton's place. Can't have empty seats around the table. I notice that the good Doctor Ellis is also here. Can we invite him to join us?

I notice Amelia is quietly standing at the back of the room and that she picks up her mobile phone and makes a short call.

The car talk has continued through all of this, and

when I tune back in, they are discussing the arcane merits of brand identity.

My eyes meet Stéphane's and I ask her about her background. She replies with a rather gorgeous French accent.

"Yes, I'm French, from Annecy, which is about 40 kilometres south of Geneve. But I've worked in Geneva, at the same compagnie as Bettina, for several years - although in a completely different division. I was recently transferred to the United Kingdom - to Exeter, in fact."

"Exeter? How so?"

"Yes, I work with geo-engineering and we use many Artificial Intelligence climate models. Exeter is well-known for its Meteorological Office, and my organisation created a department here, where we could be close."

"So, you are another one of Brant's employees?"

"Not exactly. Brant is a subsidiary of Raven Corps, and I work for the main company. I'm told it was easier to set up our company in the UK without direct affiliations to the more militaristic Brant." She steals a look toward Bettina, who was still engrossed in car-talk with the boys.

I recollect Brant has a reputation for post-war containment and reconstruction, similar to the well-known Kellogg, Brown, and Root. Brant would be hired by governments after wars and go in to clear the land and rebuild property, whilst still maintaining the peace. Iron fist in velvet glove kind of deals. Unfortunately, a string of lawsuits follows them around covering shell companies, bribes to officials, circumvention of government procurement procedures, professional negligence and even more. Meanwhile Brant was working on Artificial Intelligence weapons - including something called the RightMind combat helmet.

Stéphane gives me a broad smile, which melts my thoughts of Brant's dubious background.

"So, what do you do at Raven?" I ask. I see Lawrence Booth turn to look as well, but realise it is Stéphane's smile that has captured Booth's attention.

"Well, say a country is experiencing the bad effects of *réchauffement climatique* —crop failures or serious flooding. It could begin, perhaps unilaterally and quietly, try to modify its prevailing climate."

A whole different form of human-engineered climate change? Come to think of it, that's not such a bad idea.

"Such a project, reckons DARPA, a research arm of

America's defence department, is possible. But it could trigger chaos, and not just of the meteorological sort. It could create a 'strategic surprise'. At Raven, we have been researching how such an event might happen, and how to react to it."

I realise that the Raven relabelling is simply for show. This is deep Brant territory,

"You'll have worked out by now that I'm a scientist and part of this work is pure science—upgrading the relevant computer models to forecast changing weather patterns that could result from such an irregular geo-engineering project.

"What, so that you can spot where this could be happening?"

"Precisely. We use a branch of mathematics called *Théorie des Jeux - pardon* - game theory - to identify those countries, or even non-state entities, which might be most likely to give climate engineering a go.

"I've heard about this," I say, "Weather cannons and cloud seeding?"

"Bon. Although any attempt at unilateral geo-engineering is most likely to be limited and use a technique called stratospheric aerosol injection (SAI).

"Yes, but didn't the technique use sulphuric acid to make the rain clouds?" I ask.

"You are kind of right. The clouds are seeded with sulphur dioxide, in the upper atmosphere, to form tiny sulphate particles that would reflect sunlight back into space."

I notice several of the table are now listening to our conversation. I assume it is because of the general interest in global warming and climate catastrophe. Then she uses one of my phrases about unintended consequences.

Stéphane nods vigorously. "There are many unintended consequences of a poorly designed SAI programme. It could break down the ozone layer and give everyone harmful ultraviolet radiation. Patterns of precipitation would also change, because cooler air absorbs less moisture, and these effects would undoubtedly vary from region to region. Another problem is the acid rain that would result."

I ask, "But would it really be a force for good, or simply mask the effects of greenhouse gases rather than ending them?"

"Oui. A 'termination shock', as the injected sulphate is constantly washed out of the atmosphere in rain and snow. The closure of an SAI programme, particularly a long-lasting one, might thus cause a sudden heat jolt more difficult to deal with than the existing, gradual warming."

"But is this all fantastic conjecture?" asks Lawrence Booth.

"Non!" She replies emphatically, "A specialist game theorist organised simulations. Participants were given a variety of ideal climate outcomes and allowed to spend toy money they were given on geo-engineering projects to achieve them.

"Those who ended a round with their optimal climate outcome would then receive a pay-out of real cash. But in this game, an overabundance of SAI programmes was launched. A case of Maslow's Hammer - the law of the instrument. To make matters worse, some players tried to counter efforts at cooling, which they deemed excessive with attempts to warm the planet, resulting in a chaotic outcome creating geo-engineering wars. The conclusion was 'everybody loses.' "

I'd not heard of Maslow's Hammer but assumed it was like 'If you only have a hammer, it is tempting to treat everything as a nail."

Doctor Ellis arrives and takes his seat. I see Stéphane is now being introduced to him and switch to listening again to the car gang. Bettina is still in full flow to Hubert.

"So, what happens in 2030, when the sale of new internal combustion cars in the UK ceases? We'll be seeing a renewed emphasis on aesthetics, rather than engine character. Those foul-mouthed dinosaurs that host TV shows about cars will be superseded. No wonder they don't like electric vehicles. Car brands that rely on engineering superiority will no longer have such an advantage. Simply put, the car's power plant will no longer be the key battle ground."

"It's a designer's dream, really," I venture, "although for now, most manufacturers are opting to play it safe and to not scare the large base of traditional consumers."

Hubert speaks again, "... That's right. Why do new cars still have gear sticks and lots of dials? Some are keeping transmission tunnels and huge bonnets. These things are all superfluous. But change cannot happen overnight. It will scare the customers. Even when facing the existential crisis summoned by the looming ban on internal combustion, the automotive industry is a glacial beast not used to sudden changes of direction.

"Some will forge their own path with both chassis and top hat, while others will see the simplicity and potential cost savings of buying a platform off the shelf and then fit their own design-led bodies."

"And the others?" I ask.

Hubert answers, "Others will fall behind, producing vehicles that cannot stand apart in terms of their platform or design. Not everyone can be a winner from the race to electrification. Some big names may not pull through."

"But this is all 'shop talk' I hear Bianca say, "Surely there are other topics in this magical part of the countryside?" She looks around the table.

"Shipbuilding," I hear Clare call from the other end of the table. "We've been hearing about how 'Deesum' was once a great shipbuilding port, and all that went with it. Not just those big wooden ships, but much further back; when Dittlesham was called Dixit Ei and the Romans had established a militarised port all along the riverbanks. The road linked Dixit Ei with Isca Dumnoniorum, 'Watertown of the Dumnonii' - which later became Exeter."

"That's right," said Jago, "The Roman empire established a stronghold for its Second Augustan Legion just along the road there in Exeter. They are still unearthing Roman finds all over this county."

I realise Clare had been reading up on the area when

we took the train from London, but I was still impressed at how much she retained.

About now, I almost jump from my seat as Bianca playfully squeezes my thigh. "I'd like to talk to you after the dinner," she breathes into my ear, "Maybe outside in the garden?"

Well, how could I refuse?

9 pm.

We finish the meal. I have a growing sense of expectation concerning Bianca and the garden. Jago suggests we all have cigars, but Dr Ellis and I make our excuses and leave, with me looking quickly toward Bianca. She returns my gaze and I know I will soon be with her.

First, I must exchange pleasantries with Dr Ellis. I gather he is a physician and assumed that he was Jago's regular doctor.

"Not exactly," answers the doctor, "I was asked to come along, especially for this event."

"So, do you know someone?" I ask.

"Only in manner of speaking. Jago and I have met

previously and he suggested I might be interested in this weekend's events."

The doctor looks a little bemused by my questioning, which I think has started out in all innocence, but my journalist instinct makes me think I have stumbled upon something.

"Now, if you will excuse me," he says and strides towards another entrance to the house.

Outside, it has the soft edge of dusk. There are lights twinkling on the river and across to the other shore. Small bats flitter through the air. I can hear the ping sounds from the rigging of yachts moored in the estuary.

Then, Bianca approaches. She has wrapped herself in a stylish grey pashmina but seems to be alone.

"Lawrence has stayed to have a cigar with Hugo," she explains. "I said I'd take a walk to clear my head."

She looks at me and steps forward, "You knew, didn't you? About Jennifer Sussex and MDA - that's Miel Doux Artists? I even recognise you from that mad party with all the politicians."

Now I realise Bianca must have been present when a whole group of us attended a scandalous event in

London, at the Lanchester, with many escorts supplied by MDA.

"Jennifer never really recovered after that event, and only just escaped prison. She kept MDA going, but it is far more low-key nowadays. That's how I'm here with Lawrence."

I nod, although I still can't remember Bianca.

"Well, look, I wanted to clear the air with you so that we don't say something inopportune whilst we are both here. If Lawrence doesn't need to know, then I don't think either of us should tell him."

I nod again, and she gently kisses my cheek.

"Thank you," she says.

We both turn to go back inside but can hear two other people talking loudly. It sounds like some kind of argument.

*Less than pristine turn out of the housemaid*

Bianca and I could make out the voices of two other people in the garden. They were arguing loudly.

"It's Abigail Holbrook," I said quietly to Bianca, "But I don't recognise the man."

As if on cue, Abigail was heard by us both to say, "But Chris, you said you wanted to help. And now this has happened. What am I to think?"

Then the man's voice: "No. This is what you wanted. I never agreed."

"It must be Christopher Law," breathed Bianca. We could both see them now, the other side of a large and dense clump of box hedging. Bianca dug me in the ribs.

"We'd better go," she whispered, "Before they spot

us here. We don't want to create a scene."

I nod and we sidle away from the hedging and up a short well-mown embankment toward the house. We are soon out of earshot and our direction means that, even if we were seen, it would look as if we had come from the greenhouses and the gardener's cottage.

"I didn't expect any of the Jago's guests to be so interested in seedlings!" came a voice. We both look up and there is someone whom I take to be the gardener, accompanied by a housemaid.

"We were looking around," I reply, "We can see most of this area from my room." I look at the gardener and the slightly less than pristine turn-out of the housemaid. The gardener stretches out his hand toward me.

"Duggan, Robin Duggan, Head Gardener and this is Zoe Demelza - a student from Exeter Uni who has been working here as a housemaid. I've been showing her around the estate. Especially some of our unusual specimen plants."

I can see from Bianca's expression and then Zoe's that no-one believes what Robin has just said, but we all nod conspiratorially and let it pass.

"We are just going back to the house," says Bianca,

"We've been looking for my roving Member of Parliament - Lawrence Booth,"

"Oh, we saw him a few minutes ago. He was with that car company man and that Russian chap. They seemed pretty engrossed," answers Zoe.

I realise Zoe seems pretty bright and ask her, "Thanks, so what are you studying at Exeter?"

"Oh, robotics. Exeter has a bit of a reputation you know."

"I thought Exeter was more about mining and geology. Like the School of Mines at Imperial?" I ask.

"Oh, it is that too. But Exeter is a Russell Group university. We have an international reputation for the high quality of research and teaching. We get some of the very best academics and students from around the world, as well as investment from multinational, research intensive businesses."

Bought-in research credibility, I'm thinking, but I say nothing.

Zoe continues, "As a matter of fact, I'm hoping to get some funding after my Masters, from Brant, to further look into biological human-machine interfaces. They are making me study liberal arts first, as a precursor to machine ethics.

I'm suddenly on a kind of 'amber alert' at this finding. Human to Machine interfaces with an Artificial Intelligence component.

"Well, it has been fascinating to meet you," I say, and we leave Robin and Zoe to walk back toward the house.

I can see Lawrence Booth engrossed in conversation with Hubert Tempelmann and from a distance the body language suggests that Hubert is winning whatever point they are discussing. Bianca detaches herself from me and walks over toward Booth, just as I see Clare approaching me and then linking my arm.

"Lots to talk about," she whispers and then manoeuvres me in a different line away from Booth and Tempelmann.

*10 pm*

## *Munch*

They say that a real scream is something that passes through nature, like the one represented by Edvard Munch in his famous painting. Maybe his was a panic attack, but the shock waves reduced his face to a primal image of fear, with the sky turning blood red.

That is what we witnessed next at Magister Grange as suddenly the air was ripped apart by first one and then two shrill screams.

Two of the female servants had seen something chilling. Maisy Gill and Faith Hudson were both screaming and in a state of shock as they appeared on the stairs.

"It's Jago!" calls Faith, "He's dead in his room!"

This was one of those situations where the numbing effect of Margaritas, champagne and wine consumed over the last six hours was not replaced with crystal clear thought as new adrenaline took to my system. I can safely observe that even hearing this terrible news did nothing for my sobriety.

Instead, we falteringly tried to rationalise what had happened. It sounded as if Jago had moved back to his room and then taken his own life.

"It makes little sense," said Clare, "He seemed perfectly normal when we first met him - happy even, with the way things were going."

I nod my agreement and think back over what Jago had confided to me - about his anxiety and concerns and something related to his business.

The next action takes place in slow motion as Pascal Duret, the butler, and then Abigail Holbrook, the head of housekeeping, take to the stairs. Duret asks for Dr Ellis, who follows him toward Jago's room. Abigail Holbrook stops to comfort Faith and Maisy. I'm slightly surprised that no-one has taken Emmanuelle under their wing until I notice Clare has walked over and seems to comfort her.

I hear Emmanuelle speaking to Clare, "I was afraid of something like this. Jago has been so depressed for the last few weeks. He hid it well for the party. I don't want to go into his room until I know that a sense of décorum has been established."

I can understand this. We don't know what exactly has taken place, except that it was bad enough to have completely spooked the two maids.

Then, the doctor reappears on the landing. He moves to the edge, where the banisters create a balcony looking over the ground floor, which is where we are all standing.

Dr Ellis speaks, "It gives me great sadness to report that Jago Fox passed away this evening. It looks as if he was a troubled soul although his end seems to have come peacefully. We have contacted the police to examine him in the room where he was found. I must respectfully ask that no-one enters the room until we have been given clearance by the police"

The doctor has signalled that Jago must have gone quietly. I see Clare with Emmanuelle, but Emmanuelle's face appears to contain her grief. She speaks to Clare.

"He said one day he could imagine doing something to himself," said Emmanuelle, "and look at this."

She showed her phone to Clare, who seems taken aback.

"It's a note," she continues, "I suppose this will be evidence at the inquest."

Clare reads the note. It is an email from Jago to Emmanuelle.

*"Emmanuelle, my dearest,*

*I feel certain that I'm going mad again. I feel we can't go through another of those terrible times.*

*And I shan't recover this time. I hear voices, and I can't concentrate. So, I am doing what seems to be the best thing to do. You have given me the greatest possible happiness.*

*You have been in every way all that anyone could be. I don't think two people could have been happier until this terrible condition came along.*

*I can't fight it any longer. I know I am spoiling your life, and that without me you could work. And you will I know. You see, I can't even write this properly. I can't read.*

*What I want to say is I owe all the happiness in my life to you. You have been entirely patient with me and incredibly good. I want to say that everybody knows it. If anybody could have saved me, it would have been you.*

*Everything has gone from me but the certainty of your goodness. I can't go on spoilling your life any longer. I don't think two people could have been happier than we have been.*

*Emmanuelle, we discussed this kind of future. I want you to go ahead with the celebrations and the party. Consider it my last request.*

*Jago x"*

"It's long?" I say, almost thinking out loud.

Clare nods, "Generally, women write longer notes than men. Three or four lines by a man. Short essays and even poems, by a woman."

Dr Ellis overhears the conversation, "We should wait until we get a proper post-mortem and a police investigation. There are some things that don't stack up. First, the note itself. Why not handwritten? Then, the method of death looks like poison. He was laying on top of his bed. No sign of the note which he seems to have emailed out to everyone. Now, if it was a shotgun, or a pistol, or something with similar theatre, it would seem more likely. And here in the countryside, these kinds of weapons are hardly difficult to come by."

Clare fiddles with her own phone, "Yes - I've been sent his final words too. It seems strange that he would send them by email."

Dr Ellis concurs.

"Wait!" says Clare. "None of this makes sense. First Jago wasn't the sharpest knife in the box with computers. Yet somehow he has created an all-person bulletin which seems to have been released at the same time as his death.

"And also, The note is almost too well-written. It hasn't got the roughness one would associate with someone at the end of their tether."

Dr Ellis cuts in, "Hearing voices is often associated with mental health issues. Jago wrote he was beginning to hear voices."

Now it is Zoe's turn to speak up.

"This is weird. I'm studying Liberal Arts in Uni at present. One of the saddest things I've been covering lately is the modernist effect of Virginia Woolf on feminism."

I could hear little alarm bells ringing in my head, as if we were about to receive a lecture. But no. A revelation instead.

"Most people know Virginia committed suicide. She filled her overcoat with stones and drowned in the River Ouse. But less remember her suicide note. It is, however, kind of famous. And you know how it begins?

" '*Dearest, I feel certain that I'm going mad again. I feel we can't go through another of those terrible times.*' The same lines as Jago's. "

Zoe continues, "I can remember staring at those words, written out in Woolf's stream of writing, with scarcely a pause and no corrections. I was writing a paper about Woolf's effect on feminism. She wrote even her last words as a stream of consciousness. For my paper, I am reviewing human/machine interfaces and their ability to handle a stream of consciousness. But that letter - I found it so sad, like that scene after the desert car crash in Wild at Heart - with that girl - Sherilyn Fenn...looking for her purse. Haunting. And Virginia's note has been studied by many people."

I look at Clare. This wasn't something Jago would do. Not using a feminist tract as the basis of a suicide note. No, there would have to be another explanation.

Suddenly, we are all aware of blue flashing lights. The police arrive. I guess they want to advertise their presence because with their cars parked the lights remain flashing.

My mind is blown. Jago's death, too many Margaritas, the note, Zoe's Woolf connection and the night ablaze with red, white, and blue lights.

## *Digestif*

It is approaching midnight when two police detectives enter The Grange. They walk across to the stairs, to the same balcony that Dr Ellis had used and introduce themselves as Detective Chief Inspector Morwen Penrose and Detective Inspector Tristan Trewella.

DI Trewella continues, "Good Evening, everyone. I know what a sad and unfortunate situation we are dealing with, but now I must ask everyone to remain on the premises until we have conducted preliminary enquiries, simply to get a list of people here and your movements throughout the evening.

"I, and DCI Penrose, will need to speak to each of you alone to assist your elimination from further enquiries. It will be helpful if you can think over the events of the early evening. Who you were with, what you did and so forth."

"This sounds like a criminal investigation, to me?" says Ian Salterton.

"Yes, I am aware of that," says DCI Penrose, "We will aim to inconvenience you as little as possible, but we need to get statements from each of you."

I look toward Clare, and she sneaks a look back. We both recognise that this situation is still escalating, despite the police attempt to calm things down.

By now, Clare has spoken again to Emmanuelle, who has been told she can go into Jago's room to identify him. Emmanuelle asks that someone accompany her, and requests Clare. They have been told by Dr Ellis that the scene inside Jago's room is peaceful.

Most of the rest of the guests have been led to a separate dining room, which has been laid out with teas and coffees. This must have been the housekeeper's - Abigail Holbrook - or the party organiser's - Amelia Brophy's idea. I notice a few bottles of digestif are also circulating and think to myself that Jago would be pleased to know that the drinking had continued.

There is much police activity before Emmanuelle and Clare are called. Police in full personal protective equipment have been upstairs and into the room. I've briefly talked to Clare, who is certain that Jago's demise is not of his own doing.

I'm borderline because he confided in me that he was depressed, although he did still seem to be in fairly robust humour.

Emmanuelle and Clare are called and there is a brief dip in the conversations from those seated with coffees and brandies.

I can only wait to hear from Clare.

"

## *Lead pipe and rope*

Both DCI Penrose and DI Trewella have first gone into the library and then back upstairs to Jago's room. I start to think we are involved in an elaborate board game with lead pipe and rope. Another police officer (a constable, I believe) is organising us into an order for short interviews. We will each be alone and we understand the aim is to establish the timeline.

I'm sitting with some people who were on the second table during the dinner. As far as I can make out, they are all neighbours of Jago and live in and around about Magister Grange. There's the Woodmantons, who are a youthful, retired couple.

It turns out that Melissa Woodmanton is the owner of Woodmanton Investments, which is some kind of hedge fund. Her husband Gabriel used to be something in the city but is now retired and helps out at Milbury Moorings, which is a boatyard owned by Antonio Campbell. Then there's a Roger Ackroyd, who runs 4-Wheel-Drive adventure tours around the area. There are plenty of low-lying marshland areas and he tells me his amphibious vehicles can manoeuvre through the sand and mud revealed at low tide.

The overwhelming story I'm getting back is everyone is very shocked and cannot believe that Jago would do such a thing.

Gabriel mutters something to me:

"Of course, Jago had his share of problems, some of which seemed to be financial. He was looking for a buyer for the main company but didn't want it falling into the wrong hands. I spoke to Melissa about seeing if we could help him, but she just laughed. Jago's business and its turnover were in a different league compared to most of the businesses being run from Dittlesham."

He goes silent and I realise that Clare and Emmanuelle are returning. I look at Clare's expression.

"He looked so peaceful in his room, laid out on his bed as if he had just gone for a nap. Aside from his laptop, there was nothing to suggest he had been planning to end it all."

"He had his laptop then?" I ask, still intrigued that Jago would email a suicide note.

"We don't really know," says Emmanuelle, "It makes no sense - he seemed so happy with our engagement - this party and all."

"Are you coping?" I look to Emmanuelle. Clare has an arm around her.

"I've little choice in the matter, Jake. Jago - the love of my life - is gone and there is nothing I can do about it. I'll want justice though. I don't believe he did this and I'm almost certain that there is a hidden motive which will point to someone else."

I ask Emmanuelle, "What about that odd request at the end of Jago's note - to carry on with the party?"

"It isn't as strange as it may sound. We'd both said that if anything happened to one of us, we'd want the other to continue as normal. Like as an anti-dyadic pact."

She's got me there but sees my puzzled look: "Instead of, if one dies, we both die, we wanted the survivor to be as positive as possible. I don't know of a word for it. I just couldn't see it happening this soon."

Emmanuelle whispers, "Look, I know you and Clare

run some kind of investigation business. Would you be able to help me, do you think?"

I look at Clare, who nods, "We'll do whatever we can. But our powers are limited and we don't have any inside access to anything."

"Good," says Emmanuelle, "But I'm sure you will have -er- methods that are outside of police powers."

"As long as we don't find ourselves under arrest," I mutter.

Clare takes Emmanuelle away to her room. The rest of us all wait to be called for our interviews.

*Into the Pygtle*

The police constable has arranged the interviews in a seemingly random order. I'm about tenth to be called and I'd worked out that the interviews could only be initial ones to establish bare-bones facts.

Instead of the library, which is where I'd expected to be interviewed, I'm invited through an anteroom into the Pygtle, which is a kind of conservatory in which a couple of chairs and tables have been hastily assembled. I think the room looks like an extension of the original house, as if the original structure wasn't big enough already.

"Please, take a seat," smiles DCI Penrose.

"Can we check? You are Jake Lambers?" asks DI Trewella.

"Yes," I reply, "A visitor to this area, down from London. I came along with Clare Crafts."

The police constable then steps forward, "Thank you for allowing this conduct of a voluntary police interview. As is customary, we do not consider it necessary to provide you with legal representation. This is primarily to establish the facts and whereabouts of the party attendees on the evening of Jago Fox's death."

"I understand," I answer, "I'm not under caution and I'm free to leave at any time?"

"Correct," answers DCI Penrose, "You seem to know your law well."

"I was a journalist for several years. It is surprising what one picks up."

I am secretly wondering why the death of Jago has warranted a DCI and DI to lead the investigation. It points to something else going on.

DCI Penrose begins by asking me some basic facts about myself. How did I know Jago? How long had I known him? How long had I been in Dittlesham? Who else did I know from the party?

I could easily answer these questions. Then she asks me about the evening of Jago's death.

Had I seen anything suspicious? Were there any

strangers around? Did Jago seem to behave normally?

Again, I answer these easily. I thought it best to mention that I'd been with Bianca Hart when we'd seen Abigail Holbrook and Christopher Law outside in the garden and then later Robin Duggan and Zoe Demelza also in the grounds but didn't consider it remarkable. I explained it was around the time that cigars were being produced after the dinner.

"So, Jago was still there when you left?" asked DI Trewella.

"Yes, he was the cigar ringleader," I said.

"Was that the last time that you saw Jago?" asked DCI Penrose.

I paused, "Yes. I think it must have been. Strange, isn't it? You know; how fate deals the cards."

"Thank you, Mr Lambers. The constable will ask for your contact information in case we need to contact you further."

I looked over to where the constable was sitting by a pile of A4 papers. He clicked a biro for me to write my details.

## *Hot bodies*

Outside of the interview room, I find Clare chatting with Zoe Demelza.

"Have you two both been processed?" I ask.

"Oh yes," answers Clare, speaking for both of them, "Zoe was just telling me how she had explained to them about running into you in the garden."

"Well, that is consistent - I told them about us meeting you and Robin as well," I reply.

"Zoe was just telling me a story about Christopher Law," says Clare.

"I thought if there was ever anyone who acted suspiciously, then it would be Chris," said Zoe, "Not at first, but later he struck me as creepy."

I remember Chris was described by Jago as

'somewhat wayward and with a bad reputation' - it didn't seem so important at the time.

"Tell Jake what you just told me," said Clare.

"Well. It is embarrassing," explained Zoe, "I guess I fell for Chris in my first week here at the Grange. I later learned he was quite calculated about picking off the new student staff and looked upon the start of the academic year as so much 'fresh meat'.

"Ugh," said Clare and she visibly shivered.

"Well," began Zoe, "You know how hotels have doors that connect two rooms? It's the same here in Magister Grange, between some bedrooms.

"Chris had found me upstairs in one of the rooms and was messing around. He showed me one of the connecting room doors, but in this case, the room had been sealed off with a concrete wall. I think the master bathroom had been extended on the other side to provide a steam room or something.

"Anyway, he opened the door, and it was literally just a concrete wall.

"He joked around, 'I'm gonna lock you in! Gonna lock you in!' Then he pushed me jokingly into the space - which was probably around 40cm deep from the door to the brick wall.

"I wouldn't let him close the door so he went inside with me and said 'I'm gonna lock us both in!' And closed the door.

"I'll never forget the sound of the airtight seal and pure blackness closing.

"My hand was still on the door handle. I thought there is no way…

"But yes, it auto locked, so the door could only be opened from the outside. They hadn't bothered to disable the locking mechanism. Why would they? No-one would be stupid enough...

"Now we are stuck in a 40 cm door jamb. My feet are sideways. I can't even rotate my face from left to right without my nose squeezing against the door.

"I tell him he had better not be F*ing with me

"He says don't panic. We'll get out.

"Within 60 seconds I could feel the condensation from my body heat already dripping off the door.

"We both tried to force the door open. Nothing!

"We screamed. Nothing. The Grange was mostly empty.

"Phones? I didn't have mine, but luckily he had his. I had to get it out of his back pocket. You can imagine. It took 20 minutes to get it to be usable and all the time I was worried about it falling to the floor.

"It was a claustrophobic nightmare, and I thought I was having a panic attack. Was there enough oxygen? Would any housekeeping staff come?

"Long story short, we didn't die. We got out. We phoned Magister Grange's main desk. There was no answer. I called the gardener's cottage. Robin answered!

"I explained, 'Help us! We are stuck in Room 9!'

"Robin said 'Okay, he'd come over and find one of the housekeeping staff. A few minutes later, we heard knocking on the outside of the room's door. We screamed for help.

"Finally, after over an hour, they opened the door, and we collapsed, covered in sweat, the door dripping from the condensation of our breath and body heat.

"The entire housekeeping staff was there.

"Their response? They laughed!

"If we died in that door jamb, I'm pretty sure our corpses would still be there."

"I feel exhausted just listening to that!" I say, "I assume you fell out with Chris after that."

"I did, although I've seen him try to pick off other arrivals from the Uni, although we do at least warn them now."

"You and Robin? "I ask...

"We are just good friends," answers Zoe, "I could see you making a story out of our being together in the greenery."

We both laugh. Clare looks mystified.

"We ran into one another. I was with Bianca and Zoe was with Robin."

"Oh - and don't get any ideas about Bianca, for that matter. She arrived with the MP Lawrence Booth, and we happen to both know some of the same people."

"I'm ahead of you there," says Zoe, "I worked out that Lawrence - ex MP, by the way, was punching above his weight and must have arrived with - ahem - hired help."

"Very shrewd," sniggers Clare.

*There will be consequences*

## *Solanaceae*

Midnight and we were settled now, in a vast half-moon shaped chair in the Green Drawing Room. Why did Magister Grange have so many Drawing Rooms? There was the Green one, the White Drawing Room and another room simply called The Drawing Room. The Drawing Room also had a Boudoir attached to the back of it, which I was informed was a room just for women.

I decided we must be in the women's half of the Grange, because along the other side was a Library of mostly serious-looking and worthy leather-bound volumes and most tellingly, a Billiard Room.

"Is it okay for you to be sitting with us?" I ask Zoe, "I mean you are part of the staff here?"

"All bets are off tonight," she answers, "Look around; you'll see all the usual hierarchies have broken down. It is not every day that we lose The Lord of the Manor. Even Christopher Law is staying at the Drake Arms instead of in Magister."

I looked around and could see a dissembled group with everyone talking to one-another. The gardener, Robin, came over to join us, I suspected mainly to sit with Zoe. Jago's younger sister-in-law Cecilia was close to us. She was also a widower; her husband having died in a car crash. I realise what an unfortunate group of people I was mixing with, counting at least three spousal fatalities before Jago's demise.

I could not tell what Cecilia thought of Jago's engagement to Emmanuelle. It was clearly to her advantage that Jago should remain unmarried. And I noticed Cecilia was always very charming—not to say gushing—to Emmanuelle when they met.

I ask Clare again about how Jago had been found. Had he taken his own life? Surely, if he had done so, he would have given some hint of his state of mind earlier in the evening?

Clare had described Jago's situation in the room as peaceful. So had the doctor. No signs of frenzied alcohol drinking, just a casually placed gin and tonic, no shotguns, no drama. It was as if Jago had quietly slipped away.

But then how bizarre for him to send a note by email. He would have needed to sit down, write it, and then grapple with the email intricacies of 'delayed send', not to mention a circulation list. Then he'd have to select a time to auto-send the message. No, it wasn't something that I could ever imagine Jago doing. There had to be something criminal in play.

And why would his parting lines in the note ask that the party continue? To anyone that knew him, none of it made sense.

It made me think back to the strained conversation between Christopher Law and Abigail Holbrook.

Christopher saying to Abigail, "No. This is what you wanted. I never agreed."

What did it refer to? Could it be linked? It all seemed to happen before Jago's demise. The two of them had been walking along, side by side, their heads close together, and Abigail had been talking earnestly.

I think I can safely say that it was at this moment that a foreboding of the future first swept over me. Nothing tangible; more a premonition of the way things were settling. That earnest tête-à-tête between Christopher Law and Abigail Holbrook was ringing alarm bells.

Clare looked across to me. "None of this is right."

Zoe nodded, "I was thinking the same thing. For example, what killed Jago? Tablets? None to be seen. Violence? No sign of foul play. I can only think it was some kind of poison. Although we don't even know what Dr Ellis thinks. I assume it was something that could kill without a trace."

"That's pretty sophisticated," said Clare, "More like a Russian toxin than anything else - you know - polonium or what did they use in Breaking Bad? - Ah yes, Ricin."

"We are creeping into the mad extremes," I said, "Think about it. Where would Jago get such things? And how would he know they would work?"

"It's all too implausible," said Clare.

"Not necessarily," answered Robin, suddenly looking interested, "I used to work in Alnwick, Northumbria before I got the cottage here. There's something special about the garden in Alnwick."

"What's that?" asked Clare.

"It contains a poison garden. We gardeners were all supposed to take people for guided tours of some of the deadliest plants, which just about everyone grows in their gardens."

"Interesting," said Clare.

"Well, the original idea for the garden was to provide intrigue for visitors, who would realise how many plants could kill. The biggest killer of all was tobacco, of course, and then a few Class A drugs. But that's not the same as the deadliest, of course. That would be plants in the Solanaceae family."

"Oh, you are going technical on us!" said Zoe.

"Well, some of the more common plants in that family are the tomato, the potato, chilli and bell peppers."

"Well, we eat those a-plenty," said Clare, "And don't seem to suffer from it."

Not entirely correct, I was thinking.

"Yes, but other plants from that family include atropa belladonna and angel's trumpet."

"Belladonna - that's deadly nightshade, isn't it?"

"Correct - although belladonna - 'beautiful lady' is a misnomer. In olden times, Venetian women used the juice from its berries to enlarge their eye pupils, to make themselves more seductive."

"So it can't be that bad, then?" I ask.

"Not true, three berries are all it would take to poison and kill someone. A quicker death is assured by ingesting the root," explained Robin.

"You seem to know almost too much about this," comments Clare.

"But what about side effects - you know - symptoms?" I ask.

"The main way that it is discovered is when there are obvious giveaways like adjacent plants or berries. The poisons will run through a human system and do their damage quickly, which includes cardiac arrest.

"It doesn't sound like a pleasant way to go?" I mutter.

"Remember Romeo and Juliette? Juliette poisoned herself to induce catatonia in Shakespeare's play - that resulted from taking a belladonna potion. But that's just about all I know," says Robin.

"The gin and tonic," murmurs Clare, "It had whole juniper berries in it - do the berries of nightshade look similar?"

"Maybe slightly larger, but that's the only sign," answers Robin.

"I don't buy it," says Zoe. "Why would Jago want to go to such melodramatic trouble to poison himself? Surely an overdose of sedative would be a simpler way? - I know about this from Amy, my depressed roommate, in my first year at Uni. We helped her pull through, although she had bought a huge quantity of pentobarbital on-line for a ridiculously high price. We didn't even know how to dispose of it safely."

There was a pause, as we all reflected on what we were piecing together. We wondered how much of this the police already knew.

Then, across walks Faith Hudson, the parlourmaid. She looks over to Zoe and raises her eyebrows to attract Zoe's attention. Then, she speaks in a low voice, "Mrs Mason has called for all the staff to go to the Upper Kitchen. There is to be a briefing by Mr Duret and Ms Holbrook. I'm told that the event tomorrow continues, despite what has happened."

Several of us hear this, although we all look a little dumb struck at the thought that 'the show must go on.'

I see Clare catch Emmanuelle's eye across the room and she directly asks Emmanuelle whether this wasn't respectful.

*"Au contraire, C'est précisément ce que Jago aurait voulu!"*

My French isn't up to much but I could work out that Emmanuelle was saying it is exactly what Jago would have wanted. I could see that. And so could Clare.

Now, I look around the increasingly chaotic scene. I guess I was sobering up because the full magnitude was sinking in. We had Jago's family, invited guests, near neighbours and the staff of Magister Grange all penned in, with a couple of serious looking police detectives and a buzz of other police trying to piece together whatever was happening.

I decide I will try to speak further to the investigating officers.

## *Raggedy Groups*

The people have broken into raggedy groups. There are the car lobbyists comprising Moskvin Adam Antonovich, Bettina Kübler, Hubert Tempelmann, Lawrence Booth, and Bianca Hart. I surmise Clare and I should really be in that group.

Then there's the family and regular inhabitants of Magister Grange, Emmanuelle Catteau, Cecilia Fox, Pascal Duret, and Abigail Holbrook. I'll add family Doctor Ellis here although I can't see him at present.

Another group comprises the regular house servants: Mrs Margaret Mason, the cook; Faith Hudson, Lily Graham, Zoe Demelza and Robin Duggan.

Then, a few musicians: Joshua Harper. Drax, Jallie T and Rishi, plus their extensive and hard partying entourage.

And finally, there are the neighbours: Melissa and Gabriel Woodmanton, Antonio and Mary Campbell, Roger Ackroyd, Nat Retallick, Ian Salterton and Rose Marsh (who runs the Post Office).

It is interesting that people have fallen into these natural groupings, like so many children in their friendship circles at a birthday party.

I look around for the two police detectives, but Emmanuelle explains they left, along with Dr Ellis and Jago's body. I was expecting the whole forensics process to take considerably longer, but Emmanuelle advises me that in a case like this, they will conduct most of the examination off-site to spare the feelings of the residents.

I wonder she has not gone along.

"No. Not my scene. I'm depressed and saddened enough without going to hang around a mortuary."

I could see her point. "But how did they do that?" I ask Clare, "I mean they have moved Jago's body away with none of us noticing."

"There's a service elevator," explains Clare, "This place has been modernised, and the elevator leads directly to an external loading bay."

I decide to see who plans to leave tomorrow morning, instead of staying on for what would have been Jago and Emmanuelle's celebration. Instead, I'm stopped in my tracks by Amelia Brophy.

"You are the last two guests for me to ask," she says, "Everyone else is staying over beyond the weekend. Do you have plans to stay also?"

I look at Clare. She nods. "Yes, we'll be heading back to London on Monday - we've already got seats booked." I realise that last statement was slightly uncool. Of course, we had tickets to get on any train heading back east.

# PART TWO

*I am the one who knocks*

## *Fog of war*

I wake at seven and decide that the situation in Magister Grange is becoming like a miniature battlefield. None of us know the whole story and we are all trying to piece it together. The friction of the situation is taking over.

Like a war, the situation appears simple, but the simplest thing is difficult. The difficulties accumulate and end by producing a kind of friction that is inconceivable unless one is directly experiencing the event.

Countless minor incidents – the kind we can never really foresee – combine to lower the general level of performance, so that one always falls short of the intended goal. Iron will-power can overcome this friction ... but of course this wears down the machine as well.

Friction is the only concept that corresponds to the

factors that distinguish the real investigation from an investigation on paper. The investigation and everything else related to it is basically very simple and therefore seems easy to manage. But each part is composed of individuals, every one of whom retain their potential of friction.

This tremendous friction (like in a war) is everywhere in contact with chance and brings about effects that cannot be measured. Friction is the force that makes the apparently easy so difficult.

And all the action takes place in a kind of twilight, which, like fog or moonlight, often makes things seem grotesque and larger than they really are. Whatever is hidden from full view in this feeble light has to be guessed at by talent, or simply left to chance.

I doubt whether Carl von Clausewitz could have summarised it better.

## *Joint State Threats Assessment Team*

By mid-morning we have eaten one of Mrs Mason's incredible breakfasts. Some of us opted for the full deal, but others, like Clare and Bianca, took the light option of Muesli with wild berries.

Without fanfare, the police arrive and both Clare and I are called for a private meeting in the small anteroom which leads to the Saloon. Penrose and Trewella are both looking pretty annoyed.

DI Trewella begins:

"Good morning, Mr Lambers and Ms Crafts. You seem to know people in high places. We were both summoned to the Chief Constable for Devon and Cornwall early this morning.

"There we met Amanda Miller, who had been flown from London to Exeter by helicopter. She explained to us that Fox's apparent murder was receiving the highest-level threat assessment by JSTAT."

I noticed she referred to it as an apparent murder now.

Trewella continues, "I'll be honest, I had never heard of JSTAT."

Clare interrupts, "It's the Joint State Threats Assessment Team (JSTAT). It provides analysis on the hybrid state threats to UK interests. The security threat posed from espionage, assassination, interference in our democracy, threats to the UK's economic security and the UK's people and assets overseas."

Trewella again: "Be that as it may, she showed us various identifications and said that we were to co-operate with you in this investigation. She asked us to tell you about the other current investigation we have been involved with, which casts a shadow of doubt over what was happening at Magister Grange."

"You'd better explain," says Clare.

"It's drugs related," explains DCI Penrose, "Something involving county lines - drugs smuggled through Liverpool, sent to Manchester and then sold down here in the West Country.

She looks at both of us, "It started when a troubled teenager named Michael Snetton, then 19, operated a 'graft phone' sending out scores of text bombs to local addicts advertising heroin and crack cocaine for sale. Simply put, he had moved into the home of a vulnerable addict in Exeter and was using it as a base from where he could peddle illicit class A substances.

"Snetton, of Manchester, was careless and was arrested when police raided the address in Exeter. He was found hiding in a small broom closet in an upstairs back bedroom. Snetton initially gave a false name and was jailed for three years. Within two hours of his arrest, the drug ring was already recruiting his replacement."

DI Trewella continues, "That was another teenager named Bart Janssen, who took a train south and started using a replacement graft phone through which similar text bomb adverts were dispatched. Crazily, he thought he could just pick up the operation like running a shop."

"Janssen? Not exactly a Manchester name?" asks Clare.

Trewella answers, "No, he was originally Dutch, but has moved around. He speaks about four languages too. Dutch, French, German, and English.

Just three days after he started trading, Janssen was detained after police forced entry to the same Exeter address. Janssen gave a false name and was in possession of £4,000 cash. We think that could be the trigger for something else."

"These drug dealers are not very smart," I observe, "I mean starting the operation from the same location? I'm surprised he didn't go into the same hidey-hole!"

Trewella continues, "I know, it is incredible, but there is a further twist. After Janssen was arrested and bailed, he immediately returned to his county lines crime here in Devon, running a different phone line dubbed 'Bessie Scran'. This time he had a new phone and we think he was staying on a holiday campsite. The conspiracy took the usual form, with the text bombing of multiple Devon-based drug users offering crack cocaine and heroin. Remember, bail lasts 28 days, so he had bought himself a period of 'no harassment' from the police until he turned himself in."

"What's the trigger that you refer to?" asked Clare.

"Janssen's confession. He told us about Chaka Noon, another dealer. And that their joint source of supply seems to have been through Dittlesham," explains Trewella, "When Janssen was arrested, he realised he would be sent down for four or five years. He wanted to cut a deal with us. To admit what he knew in return for a lenient sentence. It was obvious he feared what he'd got himself into. We agreed but had to make it look as if his trial had to be stopped on a technicality. Otherwise, he would be suspected by the gang of turning State's Evidence and he would have paid heavily."

"This all sounds very irregular?" I ask.

"Oh, it is. It's the sort of situation when a police officer is embedded directly into a gang, except this time Janssen was being given a massive opportunity to start afresh, based upon what he could tell the police. We could break this entire ring."

"Fascinating, although I should stress we were originally here to visit Jago and to celebrate his engagement to Emmanuelle." I say.

"Yes, except you'd be interested to know who Janssen implied was involved with the supply of the drugs. Abigail Holbrook, Roger Ackroyd and Nat Retallick."

I'm intrigued at the mention of Abigail, but I can't quite place the other two, although I've heard their names before.

Clare interrupts, "That's Ackroyd who runs the 4-wheel adventure tours and Retallick, who runs boating holidays around the Exe?"

"Correct. I see you have a good memory, Ms Crafts," says DCI Penrose.

I'm thinking that access to four-wheel-drive vehicles and boats would be very useful for moving drugs around this area. That and Abigail Holbrook's involvement.

Clare nods, "Now we know Amanda Miller is involved, we can surely call her up to find out what she suspects?"

"I wish someone would," says DCI Penrose, "This whole situation is taking on a strange aroma and I keep thinking I'm being played."

DI Trewella looks at both Clare and I, "We were going to ask you to make some enquiries of your own. However, and I must stress this: Amanda Miller said that the investigation must look like a routine police investigation, so please don't go pulling any stunts."

We both nod our agreement.

"I feel like a trip into Dittlesham," says Chuck, "I think it's about time we paid Christopher Law a visit."

## *Flip*

An hour later we travel back along the route to Dittlesham and the driver drops us outside of the imposing entrance to The Tribute, which was an ex-coach house, and includes a 'porte cochère' (carriage porch) with what has been described as one of the largest single leaf wooden doors in the country, with another smaller door cut into it.

It now looks quite a ritzy place, with a glazed internal courtyard, with discreet tables spread around. Clare asks for Christopher, who was at a bright table in the sunlight and stood when he realised we were the ones meeting him. I was struck by how young he looked, given that he was already running corporate accounts.

"Hello," he said in a well-spoken accent, "I'll be glad to help you with what has been happening at The Grange."

I sensed Clare was on guard, although she has a

genial expression.

"We are sorry for your loss, " she adds, hurriedly.

A few introductions and an opportunity to order a light lunch. Everyone in Devon seems to eat so well, judging by the food at Magister Grange and now the choices on offer here: West-country moules marinière, Torched Lyme Bay mackerel, escabeche, saffron aioli, dressed Devon crab gratin, local braised rabbit, Hasselback potatoes, rabbit vermouth sauce - and so the list continues.

We each ordered and Chris speaks, "I guess you'll have heard things about me, but most of it is tittle-tattle. I usually live in London now, I'm a support lawyer for one of the big firms, but I've come back for a few days across when Jago and Emmanuelle were supposed to be announcing their intention to marry."

"But why stay here? Instead of Magister Grange?" I ask.

"I think if you were me, it would be self-evident. I'm away from all the gossip and can come and go as I please. There are greater expectations if one is at The Grange."

"Look, if you are really connected to the Secret Service then I guess you'll know about Jago? He confided in me several years ago, and I used to think it was 'money for old rope'.

Chris looked around the room. Aside from a small table of three women and a man, the rest of the restaurant was empty.

"Strange as it may seem, we've picked a quiet time today. I take it a table of oldies isn't anything to do with you? I even recognise Arthur over there being wined and dined by the local volunteers committee. He'll be asked to hang Christmas trees through here before you know it."

"So what can you tell us about Jago's company?" asks Clare.

"Oh, the bait," answers Chris, "Personally, I thought it was a rather elaborate scheme by Jago to hook the Russians, or whoever they are. But I can see why they thought of it, what with Jago ideally placed and all."

I realized Chris knew an awful lot about the plan to sell FST to Adam Antonovich. He also seemed relaxed talking about it to us.

"Jago discussed this with me over a couple of years. He set up the company with a 'poison pill' clause. In effect, if it is taken over, it will self-destruct. The FST poison pill is triggered when an acquiring organisation gets a certain percentage of the company's shares. It's a Flip-In Poison Pill - or as Jago called it a flippin' poison pill. It triggers after a hostile bidder acquires a certain percentage of shares and gives all shareholders, except for the hostile bidder, the right to purchase additional shares at a discount. This dilutes the shares and makes the takeover less attractive.

"That's what Jago wanted, to stop the Ikiru technology from being acquired and repurposed for evil. Like now, when they are trying to use it to make AI battle tanks or something."

Chris smiles, "There is a little bit more. The actual Ikiru chipset and its software have been transferred to another company. It is called 'Ikiru Holdings' and is a wholly owned subsidiary of FST. But there's a couple of golden shares in Ikiru, which are held by me and by Sadie Fox - Jago's sister-in-law. They provide for complete control of the direction of Ikiru, which helps prevent it falling into the wrong hands."

"How many people know about all of this? Surely the shareholders must?" asks Clare.

"Oh yes, it has all been properly documented. It just doesn't get talked about, which is how the stage gets set for the attempted bid."

Clare asks, "But what about due diligence?"

Chris answers, "There are multiple stages and the so-called hard diligence had been done. They've looked at the capitalisation of FST and at share volatility, the breadth of ownership yadda-yadda. It all comes out squeaky clean. They've run the Revenue, Profit, and Margin Trends. Over several quarters, years even, it all comes out well.

He adds, "The company's income statement will list its revenue, net income and profit. Let's just say the storefront looks terrific. It's important to monitor trends over time in a company's revenue, operating expenses, profit margins, and return on equity."

Despite his age, I can see Chris knows his stuff.

"What about competition?" asks Clare.

Chris smiles, "Ordinarily, competition would be a challenge. But size up the industry in which FST operates, and it runs rings around everyone else. Comparing the profit margins of FST with two or three of its competitors and you can see that 'competitors' is a very loose definition. It becomes obvious FST has a leader's advantage. Same with the valuation multiples. Doing something that no-one else is capable of should give an improved valuation. It certainly does!"

"And vulnerability?" asks Clare, "They seem to be a

closely knit organisation."

"It's where the weakness becomes a strength, at least at present," answers Chris, "Usually there's a tricky moment when a company is said to be founder-led. But for this technical company, a high ownership by top managers is a plus, and low ownership is a red flag. Shareholders are best served when those running the company have a vested interest in stock performance."

And the basic money flows?" asked Clare, "The balance sheet and similar?"

Chris smiles, "The consolidated balance sheet will show its assets and liabilities as well as how much cash is available and pre-existing debt is highly rated by the rating agencies. If they check the stock price history, it's all good news too."

Then Chris looks serious, "A more difficult question is of stock dilution possibilities, which is where the poison pill clause has been written, but it has been deftly buried in the paperwork. By this point, people are looking at the high expectations of profit and less at the risks (which include the delicate transfer of Ikiru to a standalone operation)

"It's all in there, but fairly well-hidden unless you now what to look for."

"In other words, it looks like a sweet deal." says Clare, smiling.

"That's what Jago, and I had hoped," answers Chris.
We both now understand Chris is a smart cookie rather than the waster and philanderer described in much of the gossip.

"They said you were staying at The Drake Arms?" asks Clare deftly changing the subject.

"I am. It's just along the road from here, but I wanted to meet somewhere where I could identify any loitering guests. You can't be too careful, as Jago has taught me. I guess you'll be leaving now? I don't want to be in here for too long, however delightful this Devon crab is." He gestured as if to pay the bill and a server walked over with a card machine.

I take the bill and pay, "We don't want you leaving unnecessary e-Trails, now do we?"

We all laugh as we made our way from the restaurant and through the door back into the bustling Dittlesham street.

*Autonomous vehicles*

After we leave the Tribute, we discover that Dittlesham's supply of taxis is limited and we have a choice to wait for a minicab, or even to walk to the Number 57 bus-stop, which would get us back to Magister Grange. We choose the minicab although it is a 15-minute wait for it to drive from Exeter to be with us.

We go back inside the Tribute, order two more coffees, sit back down at our old table, where we can discuss what we know in private.

“So, what have we got so far?" asks Clare.

"Next to nothing," I say, "And I sensed Chris seemed to be on the level."

"I agree, although you said to me you thought Jago was depressed"

I answer, "He said something about being under some kind of pressure. Commercial pressure, I think. This session at Magister Grange was supposed to resolve things."

Clare's brow furrows, "Okay, but do we know what?"

"I think it is to do with his company, inherited from his father. FST makes that Ikiru chipset for motor vehicles. There was some discussion about all of this during yesterday's dinner. It seems Brant wants to get the licence. Maybe funded by that Russian gentleman - Antonovich."

Then I remember, "They were talking about autonomous vehicles - self driving electric tanks. It sounded far-fetched to me, but now I'm beginning to wonder."

The taxi arrives more quickly than we expect. We pay the residual bill for the coffees and leave The Tribute for the second time. Then, we are driven all around the one-way-system part of Dittlesham before we get onto the now-familiar roads back to Magister Grange.

We have to change the subject during the drive back, because we are sure that the driver would enjoy overhearing our gossip about Magister Grange.

Back inside the Grange and safely in my room, Clare asks, "And who benefits if Jago is out of the picture? Not Emmanuelle?"

"No, not Emmanuelle. Unless there's a complicated Will that we don't know about I'd say it would all go to his stepson - Christopher."

Clare looks at me : "So is that a possible motive, if Jago didn't kill himself?"

I'm puzzled: "What? Jago murdered by Christopher. But why make it so elaborate? And Christopher looked so at ease discussing everything with us. No sign of jitters from a conniving murderer there!"

Clare asks, "What about the emails? It's like Jago was leaving a clear trail, but one that would be detected as false. If Zoe, the Exeter student, could recognise the email as a fake, then it won't take long for others to piece it together. By the way, I think there is more to Zoe than meets the eye."

I nod, "I agree, Zoe seems to have an instinct for this investigation, but then there is that strange conversation that Bianca and I heard. You know, between Abigail Holbrook and Christopher Law outside in the garden. Christopher was saying he'd never agreed with what Abigail wanted."

Clare asks, "So could Abigail have set something in

motion, but then Christopher was against it?"

I consider, "Maybe a contract to dispatch Jago? - But I thought everyone said that Abigail was in line to be Jago's wife, if it hadn't been for Emmanuelle?"

Clare suggests, "Let's just suppose for a moment that Christopher is short of money. That he wants to raise cash quickly. Getting control of his father's business would be a good get-rich-quick scheme."

I say, "Then, this is a stretch I know, maybe Abigail was fond of Christopher rather than Jago. There is certainly more of an age-match. And it certainly seemed that way in the garden. Abigail could want to clear the path to let her marry a potentially wealthy Christopher?"

We look at one another, "No - too cold-blooded and improbable! And if we can work this out in a few minutes, then so could the police!"

Then, there is a knock on the door.

## *Trail of evidence*

I open the door.

"Oh. My. God."

There stands an unaccompanied Amanda Miller. She is the boss of a large part of the Secret Service organisation in the UK. Someone who has asked us for help in the past. Someone who kept me in a secure location in London whilst all kinds of mayhem were breaking out in America during one of our previous adventures.

Clare looks up. "Amanda - come on in!" she shrieks, "What on earth brings you to Magister Grange?"

Amanda hugs each of us, but in her typical fashion, gets straight down to business.

"It is delicate," she begins, "and rather clandestine. I had to come to Exeter to speak to the police, and because I knew your whereabouts, I thought I'd drop by. Sorry it is rather unannounced. I'm flying back to London from Exeter in an hour, but I thought I'd owe you an explanation."

I'm thinking this must be big to get an unsolicited visit from Amanda,

"But there's no flights to London?" asks Clare.

"I'm on a military helicopter." replies Amanda.

Of course she is.

It's like one of those times when you phone someone from a plane and the other person asks, 'What's all that background noise?' ... I think the military helicopter explanation wins.

"So, here's the thing," begins Amanda, "Things are not quite as they seem."

I had a sudden inkling that I knew what she was about to say.

"Jago Fox worked for us. For SI6."

Not that. I was not expecting that.

Amanda continues, "Jago has been involved in breaking a Russian gangster ring. He has been an embedded agent for many years."

I could see Clare leaning forward in her chair - a look of disbelief on her face.

"But Jago...? He's well, not the most obvious candidate!" she utters.

"Exactly. When did you ever hear of a spy being 'obvious?' "

"So, was he killed by the Russians?" ask Clare, "Assassinated with a spray-on nerve agent?"

"Not exactly. There's a strange twist to this story," answers Amanda.

I knew it.

"Jago is still alive. Like Shakespeare's Juliet, he faked his own death and left a confused trail of evidence. It's why we had to remove his 'body' so quickly from the scene. Ably assisted by Dr Ellis who we sent in to make sure Jago's story would hold."

I said I knew it. Dr Ellis must have been a plant to assist the cover-up.

"Wait. Jago is alive?" asks Clare. "Does Emmanuelle know?"

"Jago is in London now, in the very offices that you, Jake, had to inhabit all that time ago."

I thought back to when Amanda had offered me some protection whilst Bigsy, Clare and Chuck Manners were looking for missiles in the Arizona desert.

"Why?" asked Clare.

"We think Jago's cover had gone. Yet he was on route to discovering a huge Russian armaments deal. Someone, we don't know who, has been sent to assassinate him during the party. We have just made it either inconvenient for them or else incredibly fortunate."

"Do the police know any of this?" I ask.

"Nothing. They will go about their investigation, although Jago's missing body may give them a few headaches. Doctor Ellis helped with the rather unusual arrangements."

I knew it.

"So does this mean that Jago has given his assassins the slip?" ask Clare, "But at the cost of his entire lifestyle."

"Agreed, although Jago is a man of many parts,"

smiles Amanda, "His Will transfers control to Christopher, but the company has already been reformed into a public–private partnership.

"But I thought they were old hat?" I ask, "Something from the late 20th Century?"

Amanda answers, "PPP covers hundreds of different long-term contracts with a wide range of risk allocations, funding arrangements, and transparency requirements.

"To use the OECD definition, it is a 'long term contractual arrangement between the government and a private partner whereby the latter delivers and funds public services using a capital asset, sharing the associated risks'."

"So, Jago's hands are tied?" asks Clare, "And the government has some control of the company?"

"Oh yes, but it is to one of the most lucrative money streams available, and he is well-hidden in the P3 structure of private entity financing, construction, and management of a project. In return he gets a promised stream of payments directly from the government."

Amanda smiles.

"But what about Emmanuelle? They were supposed

to be getting engaged... tonight!" asks Clare.

Amanda answers, "Emmanuelle's dual nationality serves well here. If she reverts to her original name - Barbet? - And reapplies for her Canadian citizenship, we can pull all the strings. She could be Canadian by tomorrow."

"But the house?" I ask, "Magister Grange."

Amanda answers, "It was always in the arrangement with Jago. We arranged a deal. A property swap. Jago donates his property to the UK Government. It will be ideal as an annex to the Royal Marine Commando training site 3-4 miles along the River Exe at Lympstone. In return, he gets a beautiful heritage property in Metro Vancouver. It is so close to Emmanuelle's old stomping grounds and in a delightful area with a very mixed and gracious lifestyle."

"But Emmanuelle's existing property next door to Magister? Seymour Court?"

"She keeps it. A useful Devonshire bolthole. I wouldn't advise Jago to visit at least until he has revised his appearance somewhat."

Amanda says, "Jago knew something like this could happen. He has to think of it as a change of job. Except he is keeping his pay from his last job. And probably upgrading his lifestyle. There are plenty of big ticks in boxes with this career change."

"So, does Emmanuelle know about any of this?" asked Clare.

"Not from us, although I suspect Jago told her some of it, but we'll want to keep this close for at least another week."

I realised she meant until after Jago's funeral.

## *I'm reviewing the situation*

*I'm reviewing the situation,*
*I must quickly look up ev'ryone I know.*
*Titled people -- with a station*
*Who can help me make a real impressive show!*

*I will own a suite at Claridge's,*
*And run a fleet of carriages,*
*And wave at all the duchesses*
*With friendliness, as much as is*
*Befitting of my new estate...*

*"Good morrow to you, magistrate!" Oh gawd!*
*I think I'd better think it out again.*

Lionel Bart / Eric Rogers

## *Wannabee*

Clare and I are alone in the bedroom. Amanda has left and is probably almost back in London by now. I swirl a cup of cold coffee.

"So now what?" I ask Clare.

"I guess we should find out what Emmanuelle knows; she certainly gave nothing away yesterday."

"And what about the armament deal? Is it still being discussed?" I ask, "It makes sense that Adam Antonovich, Bettina Kübler and Hubert Tempelmann remained close, maybe also with that dodgy ex-MP - you know - the lobbyist - Lawrence Booth."

"I'm trying to work out the wannabe assassin," says Clare. "It can't be any of the top table car industry guests, nor Cecilia Fox, Dr Ellis, our pop stars Drax and Josh, neither can it be Lawrence Booth and

Bianca Hart."

I suggest, "What about the neighbours? Neither Melissa and Gabriel Woodmanton nor Antonio and Mary Campbell seem very plausible. The postmistress? - Rose Marsh - I don't think so."

Clare adds, "Then there's the staff...Pascal Duret - the long-time loyal butler. Margaret Mason, the cook, and Faith, Maisy, Lily and Zoe all maids on contract."

I say, "We should hold on to that thought regarding the maids. Short term hires, maybe one of them has been put up to something?"

Clare asks, "Who does that leave? That we've skipped over? A major roll call of suspects...Christopher Law - a cool operator except for that exchange with Abigail. Amelia Brophy - the mystery woman and party organiser. Ian Salterton - the out-of-shape drunken book author."

I say: "Out-of-shape reminds me of the opposite. We have several guests who have the fitness worthy of an assassin. There's Roger Ackroyd - who runs the off-road adventure tours. Nat Retallick who runs the boating holidays. Penelope Richards, who grows vines, and looks the very model of outdoor fitness.

Clare adds: "And two more we still haven't

mentioned: Abigail Holbrook - apparent lover to Christopher. And Robin Duggan the gardener."

I can see that Clare has been writing all of this down.

"What about if it has been contracted out?" Maybe someone from the top table hired someone else to do the deed?"

"Agreed, except what we now know is that Jago beat them to it. He staged his own death before the real assassin could make a move."

"But how would Jago get the intelligence to know that he had been rumbled?"

We both stare at the wall for what seems like minutes.

Clare begins, "Suppose...Suppose the walls have ears?"

Now Clare has me anxious.

"Seriously, if there was a hidden alcove where Chris trapped Zoe, then there's a strong possibility that there are other hidden passages. You know, used by servants, or as a hiding place - like an early form of Panic Room."

"Who would know about this?" I ask.

"I suppose the butler and the housekeeper are the most likely Pascal Duret and Abigail Holbrook."

Clare pauses, "Shall we tell the police what we think?"

"Just about the secret passages. Nothing else, though."

## *Pursuivants*

We leave my room and make our way back downstairs. I can see that there is animated preparation for the evening's event. I'm still quite taken aback that Emmanuelle wants it to go ahead, although none of the other guests seem to think it unusual. Maybe the champagne has relaxed everyone's critical thought.

Clare and I approach DCI Morwen Penrose and DI Tristram Trewella. They both appear to be a little 'off' with us, which we decide is because we seem to have ruffled feathers because of their boss being called upon by SI6.

"You'd better come on through to our temporary office," says DCI Penrose. She shows us through to another anteroom. This one is close to the Billiard Room and has been prepared as a makeshift crime scene office.

"Your boss seemed very assertive," says DCI Penrose, "I assume there is more to both of you than meets the eye."

"Yes, but we really did not know we were getting into something like this when we came down here for what we thought was an engagement party, " answers Clare.

"Amanda Miller says she is sending someone else to oversee the security aspects of what is happening here," answers DCI Penrose, "He's an American - his name is Chuck Manners. He is being sent to the military base along the river this afternoon and will be driven from there to Magister Grange."

Clare and I look at one another. "We both know Chuck. In fact, we have worked with him in the past. What did Ms Miller say?" I ask. I'm already thinking that if Chuck is being flown in, then there must be quite something at stake.

DCI Penrose shrugs and then answers my question, "Ms Miller said little really, simply that Chuck was a useful asset to have in a situation like this. She clarified we should be seen to continue to run the investigation, but that we could expect considerable help from Mr Manners and from both of you."

I answer, "Well, we have one thought, which is

probably better investigated by you. We think that the Grange may have a secret concealed passage, probably on the first floor."

"We are ahead of you there, " says DCI Penrose. "Mrs Mason, the cook, has already told us about the linking passages that run behind the rooms on the first floor. It was originally a series of linked priest holes but then converted into a servant passageway."

DI Trewella adds, "The original construction of the Grange dates back to the 16th Century when religious beliefs could be a matter of life and death. Religion, politics and the monarchy were at the heart of how England was governed."

Trewella continues, "I was brought up in a Catholic household and we used to study the violent history of the Catholics and Protestants.

"In the 16th Century, the Catholics had such power that when King Henry VIII sought annulment of his marriage to Catherine of Aragon, the Pope refused.

Trewella is on a roll: "To cut a long story short, Henry split from the Catholic Church and founded the Church of England. Later, Queen Mary took England back into the Catholic Church and anyone who refused to give up their Protestant beliefs was burned at the stake, earning Mary the nickname

'Bloody Mary.'

"Mary was succeeded by her sister Queen Elizabeth I, who wanted a strong, independent England with its own religion, trade and foreign policy. She restored the Church of England and all who did not conform were fined or imprisoned."

The twists and turns of a royal Britain.

Trewella adds, "Now the scariest part: It was made High Treason for a Catholic priest to even enter England and anyone found aiding and abetting a priest would be punished. To this end 'priest hunters' or 'pursuivants' were tasked to collect information and locate any such priests. That's how the priest holes came about to conceal Catholic priests."

"No stone left unturned, " I say.

"Truly a matter of life and death," says Trewella.

"And nowadays also a way to access rooms on the first floor, if you know about the linking passages," says Clare.

Linking passages, priest hunters, Jago's unannounced return. A mystery assassin. I have an overwhelming need to get outside of the house for a while. Get some fresh air to clear my mind.

I walk back out into the garden, where everything has changed.

## *Rigid Inflatable*

A stage has been erected on the land which leads down toward the water. It has been set up with a broad apron from which one assumes the whole of Dittlesham could watch the concert. In the distance, just before the start of the vineyard, is a control point, which I can see is where the band's sound and lights will be mixed. Around me small trucks like souped-up golf carts buzz, bringing more equipment to the site. I realise that the combined capabilities of Drax and Jallie T's technician Rishi mean we will soon have a festival quality venue created on site in Magister. No wonder there was so much pressure for it to go ahead.

Then, an American accent calls across, "Jake Lambers!"

I turn to see Chuck Manners already scooping Clare into his left arm.

"This must be a big deal, to have you flown down from London, into the Marine camp and then ferried here!" says Clare.

"Ferried is the right word, too! The boys in the Marine base asked me if I'd like a ride on their RIB, so I came along the last part by river. They brought two of their crafts and kindly left one at my disposal. Quite a welcome!" answered Chuck.

Chuck adds, "Rigid Inflatable Boat - Marine vessel of choice and so manoeuvrable and fast. It's more like an Offshore Racing Craft than a mere dingy. Diesel-powered waterjets for propulsion with immense power. They never told me that Devon would be so much fun."

"Okay, Chuck, we're going to pull you away from the crowd to ask you what on earth is going on."

Chuck smiles, "It's never dull when we get together, is it?"

He continues, "First up: The tank-mad Russians want to buy their way into the inventions of Jago's company. They are trying to seal a deal with the mercenary Brant organisation. They think it would give them control of battlefield management.

"Then, if they pay for the company, Christopher Law gets to make a huge amount of money. As do financier Adam Antonovich and scientist Bettina Kübler. And also, incidentally, if Chris Law marries Abigail Holbrook, she will also do well out of it."

"Who was running the hit on Jago?" asks Clare. "I assume Amanda has you well briefed on the situation?"

"Oh, yes...It was my idea to stage Jago's demise. To draw out the bad people," says Chuck.

"We've made a list of suspects," I explain, "Graded into different categories."

Chuck smiles, "We really need a little something up our sleeve for tonight's celebration. Something that should flush out the bad actors."

"Actors?" says Clare, realising that Chuck has slipped into spy-speak.

"Yes, there's more than one person here with an interest in a 'Jago-free' outcome," says Chuck.

*Channelling Coachella*

The car event in Exeter must be some big deal because they are ferrying the guests to the much concert in multiple ways. There are motor coaches to the front door of Magister, a limo service, and then, on the river a large blue and yellow party boat ferrying people to Magister Grange's landing stage. Not forgetting the helicopter shuttles, which I assume are for the VVIPs.

I see Bianca outside, looking at the unfolding rock concert around her. She hurriedly gestures for me to come over to her and I pull Clare along with me. Bianca is wearing festival clothing now, blue wide-flared jeans, a wide buckled belt. Fringed light brown leather jacket and black hair tumbling down over her shoulders. I'm thinking she is channelling Coachella more than Exeter.

"Extensions!" whispers Clare as we walk over. Then loudly, "Bianca, what is it?"

We both observe Bianca's worried expression.

"Well, after yesterday's wine soaking, I wanted to apologise to Salterton. Although, with my new hindsight, I think he had it coming."

"I get the impression that he was over-tactile?" asks Clare.

"Yes, although I now realise it was all part of a bigger plan."

Clare and I look at one another. We can't guess what Bianca is about to say.

"To start with, I thought he was just rather fresh with me," says Bianca, "I went to his room, to apologise, you know, for tipping wine on him and getting him removed from the table."

We both nod, wondering what could happen next.

"Well, I'm used to dealing with men, so a visit to his room didn't faze me. For protection, I usually carry a small canister of Mace in my bag, and I have one of those defender rings too."

I consider this. Clare carries nothing like that, although, I suppose in fairness, I've known Christina Nott carry an automatic weapon in her

Mulberry.

Bianca continues, "He was on the phone when I arrived and gestured for me to come in. Considering what had happened, I was relieved to see he was all smiles."

"His room was quite large, more like a studio, with a bed area and a separate sitting area. The areas were divided by a clever metal divider, which broke up the space and still let light through from the window, which was on the bed side of the room. As Salterton was in the bed area, I slipped into the sitting area, which was also close to the main door to the room.

"He indicated he would only be a couple of minutes and continued his phone conversation. It seemed to be with Amelia Brophy - you remember - the party organiser."

"Well, I sat on a chair waiting and could see a black plastic box protruding from under a table in the corner of the room. It was about the size of a small travel makeup box. I had nothing to do, so I rather casually flicked it open.

"It looked at first like it was holding rows of batteries, but then I realised they were actually gun cartridges. There were more than 50 and seemed to be arranged in neat rows by size. I even kept one. I put it in my bag."

"I hurriedly flicked the case shut again and used my foot to push it back under the table. Then I spotted a longer bag. I assumed it must have a rifle in it. That was when Salterton walked around the edge of the bed and into the sitting area. He could see me looking at the bag."

"He spoke, 'Ah - I see you are looking at my fishing bag. The Exe has several good places for line fishing for salmon, trout, and grayling. But you have to be a member of RETA (That's the River Exe and Tributaries Association). Then it's £30 a day for salmon and £10 a day for trout.

"But I doubt that is why you are here?"

Bianca continues, "I shook my head, 'No. I wanted to apologise. For throwing that rather good wine all over you. I guess your hands may have slipped onto my leg and I over-reacted?'

"No, It was my fault," Salterton replies " I fully deserved to be thrown out of that event after my misconduct. I hope my apology here is sufficient. I didn't want to come to find you in case you thought - well - you know - the worst. But I wrote you an apology and was planning to pop it under your door later."

He looked through his jacket, which was hanging from a chair and produced a small piece of folded paper.

" 'Here - you see,' "

"I looked at the paper, which had an apology on it.

*"My Dearest Bianca,*

*I don't know what came over me. Too much wine, I fear. Sorry for spoilling the evening for you.*

*Ian Salterton."*

"I looked at the note. It was certainly short, but to the point. And I wondered. If Ian Salterton was an author, his spelling or typing didn't seem to be too good. He'd spelled spoiling with two 'l's. I said nothing, though. I was supposed to be in the middle of an apology."

Bianca pauses, looks at us both and says, "I know I can trust you, right? Only I'm almost certain that Salterton wanted to get thrown out of the dinner. I think he needed to do something that he knew would rile me sufficiently that I'd react and then he'd be asked to leave."

There was a sudden 'crumpf' noise ahead of us. We all look up. It was the Public Address system starting up.

Rishi was on stage. They had made him the announcer, at least for the first part of the event. Then I realise they had enlisted Jallie T as a support act. This promised to be some show.

"We'll hold those thoughts, Bianca, " I say, "Only I think it is about to get rather hectic around here."

Little did I know.

## *An instinctive form of theatre*

DEVON NEWSCAST - Polly Violet.

Exeter didn't know it had been waiting for this gig. Dittlesham certainly didn't. Announced just last week to feverish anticipation, this show in the tiny town of Dittlesham is the first maximum energy stadium rock show by international artists seen in the West since forever. As his agent revealed, Drax will not stick around to play the rest of the West Country although he plans to return later for a full-fledged tour.

Incredibly, this set was specially created for this one show. By good fortune, Joshua Harper, the lead guitarist of Canadian band Erebus was in town as was the singer Jallie T. The occasion - the engagement party of Jago Fox and Emmanuelle Catteau - thrown open to the locals with all invitations by word of mouth.

'Now' makes a fitting opener to the set: 'Times like now you learn to live again / Times like now you give and give again,' Drax struts although dimming the track's usual biting energy for a more intimate intro. 'The Great and the Small' follows to rapturous acclaim, horns thrust high as Drax and his cohort thrash away like their lives depend on it.

Then a slower rap mix - featuring Jallie T. I can't swear, but I think it morphed into a Christina Nott cover 'Strobe me till I chant' which Jallie T took away like an express train.

Then another new song 'The horizon is a beltway' from an Erebus album, which sees Erebus guitarist Josh take to the stage with the guitar solo played with meteoric aplomb. Drax gives his all in the next three songs which are recent cuts from his last album but rejigged with the Erebus guitar and Jallie T's supplementary vocals.

At the core of Drax's one-and-a-half-hour set is an instinctive theatricality. They've got them all nailed down to a T, each beat walloping and each lick soaring – they're unashamedly over-the-top in their performance, but it's testament to Drax's inimitable artistry that even when three-minute songs are blown out to epics that go past the 10-minute mark, it never feels excessive or boastful, and gives his two guest performers room to breathe, even in what is turning into a squally evening, but one the hardy westerners simply don't notice.

As the night starts to wind up, the rain stops as suddenly as it started and Drax plucks an ultimate rarity, riffing on Nirvana's Teen Spirit - which Jallie T had worked with Christina Nott in their recent global tour. We are in supergroup territory here and I have to pinch myself to remember this is being played out at a private party on the shore of the River Exe, with the audience comprised of mainly locals from east of Exeter.

We end on the one-two punch of Drax's 'Lost' and 'Skip.' The band close out with a mesmerising display of fireworks which seems to have been aimed at Powderham Castle on the other side of the Exe. Like this shore was saying to Powderham 'Follow That'.

Afterwards, leaving the gig, it's hard not to feel like we've just witnessed a historical event. Mother Nature may have brought rain and the ground may slope up from the river, but Drax and his accomplices came in even harder with their thunder.

*Small insect on jacket*

It was difficult - no impossible - to hold conversations during the concert. Aside from it being exceptional, it was also very loud, so it was as if everything we had been discussing had been frozen for a couple of hours while Drax and the hastily formed supergroup played.

We were standing in a small group watching the show. There was Lawrence Booth, Bianca, Salterton, Clare and I. Slightly awkward having Salterton and Booth together, although Booth didn't seem to notice.

"Amazing!" says Clare as the final echo pulsed back from the Haldon Hills across the river.

"Hmm, it should make Powderham think about its next concert!" says Ian Salterton, who was now standing with us. I instinctively look for his hands and feel slightly ashamed that it was almost a reflex action.

Salterton is looking towards me when I think I see a small insect on his jacket. I realise it is a tiny, ragged hole.

Then, with a surprised look in his face, Salterton keels over, backwards, making no attempt to cushion the fall.

"Oh my God!" says Clare, "He's been shot."

Those of us near Salterton instinctively dive to the ground and my shame and embarrassment from moments ago turns to fear as I'm now hiding on the ground from a sniper bullet.

There is a silence and I can see an area of the crowd parting as two things happen.

First, I see people taking cover like some organic crop circle and then I see the strange sight of Chuck Manners running toward three parked vehicles. A Jeep Renegade, a Claas Arion 660 tractor and a small Club Car 1500 All-Wheel Drive.

I'm expecting Chuck to leap into the Jeep, but he moves onto the Club Car. Okay, it is not the kind they use at golf courses, but its heritage is clearly with the tartan clad. I wonder what Chuck is doing, but then I realise it was the easiest vehicle to steal. It had keys in it and he is manoeuvring it through the crowd and down a slope, past a vineyard and toward the River Exe.

Now I can see he is in pursuit of someone, but I can see and hear, in the distance, the second RIB, which was loaned by the marines to Chuck. Someone is in it and it is making good speed across the River Exe. I guess at this point the river is wider than a mile, but even longer to cross because of the sand banks.

The RIB is well on its way across the river when I see a new break in the crowd as Chuck returns with the Club Car.

"She had too much distance!" he says, "There was no way I could catch her, and she made it even worse by stealing my boat! It will be most embarrassing to admit that to the Marines."

He looks over to Salterton, on the ground, being tended by several people, including, by now, Dr Ellis, a couple of festival-support Paramedics, and DCI Penrose and DI Trewella.

To my astonishment, Salterton was being pulled to his feet. I could still see the tiniest of holes in his jacket, but then I realised he must have been wearing body armour.

Sure enough, DI Trewella picked at Salterton's

clothes and soon revealed a ballistic vest, which I assume was made of Kevlar. On it, at chest height, was a small indentation. A bullet had been stopped from piercing the vest although I could imagine it must have created a huge bruise on Salterton. The obvious question sprang to mind; How did Salterton know to be wearing such protection?

Once Salterton could walk, he was hurried away to an inside room at the Grange, with a close escort from Penrose, Trewella and Chuck Manners.

Clare gestured to me to follow, and a group of us were soon assembled in the same room that the detectives had used for our interviews. The two detectives seemed at ease that we were present with Chuck Manners.

They questioned Lawrence Booth's and Bianca Hart's presence, but I chipped in that we thought Bianca had some critical evidence.

Trewella asked Booth and Dr Ellis to leave the room.

As the door closed, Salterton began, "Alright, I know, we need to cut a deal. I'll turn State Evidence, but it will be in return for protection. SOCPA - Immunity."

He seemed to be ahead of the two local police, although Chuck Manners knew the right responses.

Chuck began, "Serious Organised Crime and Police Act 2005 (SOCPA) may be used by prosecutors to secure intelligence or evidence from offenders to assist in an investigation or prosecution."

Salterton nodded wearily. I had a sense that he had travelled this path before.

"I'll want an immunity notice to be recorded by the DPP - Director of Public Prosecutions. And - to avoid doubt, I know that there is something amiss with the reported death of Jago Fox. There are too many additional people buzzing around this situation."

He was right, of course, although I doubted we'd give him the satisfaction of knowing the truth about Jago.

"You have a chance to get this whole thing waived, but you need to tell us everything," says Chuck Manners. I could see that Chuck was used to this kind of negotiation among professionals.

This was all moving along faster than Penrose and Trewella's comprehension.

Chuck helpfully summarises.

"It's not so difficult. You were sent here to

assassinate Jago Fox. Something happened to Jago before you could act. The commissioners of your attempt wanted you out of the picture and so attempted to kill you with a highly professional long-range sniper bullet."

But someone had warned you," intervenes Penrose, "They had told you to wear protection until you could leave here."

"Is this related to the drug smuggling?" asks Trewella.

"Drugs smuggling?" asks Salterton, looking confused. He looks at Clare, then me, as if wondering where the drugs questions are coming from.

Chuck gives him a line, "Yes, don't deny it. You were tied up with the drug operation being run from Magister Grange."

Salterton responds, now aware of the line of suspicion picked up from Chuck.

"Oh yes, the drug smuggling. I suppose that could get someone like me killed."

I realise that Chuck and now Salterton are trying to deflect the questioning away from the real subject of the possible sale of FST.

"And what about the sniper? The one who shot at you? You said 'She', Chuck. Who was it?" asks Trewella.

"Someone I've seen before, " answers Chuck, "Although not in quite the same way. It was Amelia Brophy."

The party organiser...Handy with a sniper rifle?

"Yeah, I thought I recognised Amelia when I first arrived. But there was a difference. I knew her as Sean Brophy, a professional hit man around ten years ago."

"What, so she took a walk on the wild side?" asked Clare, incredulous.

"More than just shaving her legs so he was a she," answered Chuck, "She paid plenty for that makeover."

"Well, I knew Amelia was wiry fit," said Clare.

I nodded. Although I was having to get used to the thought that Amelia could handle a sniper rifle.

"Bianca," I asked, "Do you still have that cartridge?"

She riffled through her bag and produced a slim brass cartridge with a copper-coloured tip.

Chuck reached across and looked at it. " Winchester style, M118 Long Range," He said, "Look see the stamping on the end of the cartridge case?"

I looked but could only see 'LC 95 LR'.

"These are sniper munitions, "said Chuck, "Put this into an M24 SWS and it'll remain supersonic for 600 metres."

"SWS?" I ask.

"Sniper Weapon System," answers Chuck, "Mr Salterton was lucky it was not an anti-material rifle like an M82, or the bullet would have passed through his Kevlar with ease. I can see why the sniper brought an M24, because there are so many of them out in the wild, mainly supplied by the American military."

We all turn to look at the cartridge. A thin casing around 10 centimetres long with the small sharp tip of a bullet.

"Salterton, you were so lucky," said Chuck.

"You'd better check my room," says Salterton, "I think I know where this is heading."

Penrose gestures to Trewella and he gathers another

policeman and the two of them leave the room. I guess they are going to check out Salterton's room.

A radio crackles. "We've found the weapon," comes a scratchy message, "In Salterton's room."

"Don't touch anything," orders Penrose and exchanges a look with Chuck.

Chuck says, "Yes, better to preserve any evidence, although this will look as if it is Salterton's own weapon that shot him. Something else to figure out."

*Don't cross the streams*

*Don't cross the Streams...It would be bad*

*Egon Spengler, Sedgewick Hotel,*

## *Pace*

Sunday, and we've all enjoyed another of Mrs Mason's breakfasts, supplied late because of the excitement of the concert and the poor attempt to stifle Ian Salterton. I consider the missing guests. We've lost Jago Fox, Ian Salterton held in custody and Amelia Brophy, the escaped failed assassin.

The two detectives have now moved into The Grange and are sitting together quietly, discussing the events of the last two days. I can't work out if there should be a stronger protocol surrounding their investigation.

I'm sitting with Clare and Chuck. We have formed our own breakaway detective club and are still trying to make sense of what we have seen.

She gestures to a small group sitting together at an adjacent table. "The businesspeople still look as if they are trying to cut a tank deal," says Clare.

"Funded with Russian money," adds Chuck.

"And utterly ruthless," I add.

"The police..." muses Chuck, "I'm not sure they have got a grip on this. They've interviewed everyone but seem to be completely blind-sided about the shot fired towards Salterton."

"It's PACE, " suggests Clare, "You know - The Police and Criminal Evidence Act which provides codes of practice for the exercise of powers by the police."

"Yes, I know about PACE and its modifications," says Chuck, "A fairly wide-ranging piece of legislation, because it deals with police powers to search an individual or premises like Magister Grange, including their powers to gain entry to those premises, the handling of exhibits seized from those searches, and the treatment of suspects once they are in custody, including being interviewed."

"But we're not in custody?" I ask.

"No, it's been cleverly played. Everyone has been asked to stay here until Monday and are doing so of their own free will. Leaving early would simply mark us out as suspicious. Well, not us exactly, but most people."

He adds, "When PACE created Codes of Practice, it changed the rules in these types of investigations. It replaced nearly all pre-existing powers of arrest. Here we have a presumed suicide or murder in a stately home, followed by a second attempt on someone's life. With all the suspects in the same house, it's no wonder that the police are taking a liberal interpretation of the Act."

That's when Clare's phone rang.

She answers it, says hello, and then goes silent, listening to the caller.

"The Drake Arms," she finally says, "At 1pm. We can do that. It will be me, Lambers and Manners. Yes, no-one else."

She looks back to me, "Amelia Brophy wants to meet us. This afternoon. She says no police and no strong-arm tactics or she will disappear."

## *M24*

Chuck, Clare, and I take the short taxi ride to the centre of Dittlesham. By now we can confidently describe it as a small, picturesque town on the outskirts of Exeter on the east bank of the Exe estuary.

In the past, it was a busy port and much of its history is still evident in the architecture and layout that gives it a distinctive maritime trader identity.

There was much bustle and it was obvious that Dittlesham has much to offer with boutique shops, riverside walks, bird watching, sailing, moorings, cafés, restaurants and inns, little parks, a quay-side antiques trader, and a museum. There were certainly a good number of well-heeled folks around and business looked brisk.

The taxi driver had driven us to the Quayside, although when we asked about our destination, he looked surprised and said we would need to go around the whole road system again because everything was one-way in the heart of Dittlesham.

We start our second lap and Clare observes, "It is easy to see how Salterton became 'plugged in' to the place." She was looking at the differing architectural styles of Dutch gable houses reflecting its maritime past, Georgian and Edwardian houses, Victorian terraces, cottages, and a few unique modern properties.

"Just look at these small streets. I doubt whether modern cars will even fit along some of them," she adds.

"No wonder it is a one-way system," says Chuck, "I don't know what it will be like if you Brits ever get American-sized cars!"

"It's a curious place to meet Amelia, then," I muse, "I mean, she is pretty much trapped in here."

We are once more being driven along the main Fore Street and the taxi this time stops us outside of a large pub, which I assume was once a coaching inn. As we cross the one-way street, I could see a small courtyard, with a raised casual seating area. A few bicycles are propped along one edge. Large, triangular and tan-coloured, umbrellas reminiscent of sails cover the tables. In the far corner was sits Amelia Brophy, apparently alone.

We walk towards her. She wears a dark, understated jacket and black jeans. I suddenly realise that she could look quite boyish and wonder if it is part of her ability to operate as a chameleon.

"Thank you for coming," she says, "I've thrown them off the trail. They think I am in London now. But I'm realistic that I've only bought limited time."

I thought this was an interesting way to start the conversation, although Chuck wanted to move it along.

"Who are you working for? You'll need to tell us if you expect any help. We can make you disappear, far better than you can doing it your way. And once you've gone, we won't care about you any longer, which is more than can be said for your current employers."

"That's fair," she says.

I was amazed at how these professional agents would talk to one another on the level. It wasn't like in the movies where one of them would be pointing a weapon of mass destruction at some sensitive part of the other person being questioned.

"I've been working for the Russians, but you knew that already," she answers, "They botched this situation. Sending that bungler Salterton. Honestly. He was a liability from the start. Then my employer realised their mistake and asked me to remove Salterton from further engagement."

"An interesting touch, shooting him with his own weapon, " observes Chuck.

"Yes, even that was lame. He was using a standard issue American M24. I know they have the velocity but using it with standard ammunition! If Salterton had been wearing Kevlar, the munitions wouldn't penetrate. No, I was expecting an M82 anti-material weapon, or even an M95. Something that would break through whatever Salterton was wearing.

It all sounded so cold blooded, as she spoke.

Amelia continues, "Despite my perfect shot to his body, I expect he is still alive. I saw him go down but didn't stay around to watch the aftermath. Now I need to lose the Russians, who will be interested in settling the account."

"Why use his weapon?" asks Clare.

"Convenience. I knew he had brought ordnance to his room. He comically disguised it in a fishing rod bag. Really. Using his own weapon against him would confuse all the increasing number of sleuths in Magister Grange. It also pointed to a likely culprit for Jago Fox's murder, if they are looking in that direction."

I keep reminding myself not to mention that Jago is still alive. It is getting more complicated now there two people in this condition.

Brophy looks at each of us. "I can see from your reactions that Salterton must still be alive. I suppose you are cutting a deal with him, too?"

Okay - she has figured out that Salterton lives. She would make a brilliant poker player.

"So now it gets more complicated. The Russian lead for this assignment was Moskvin Adam Antonovich. He is doubly annoyed now. First with Salterton for botching his assignment and second with me for not finishing off Salterton.

She continues, "The Russian spin on saving face is to punish those who make one lose face. The Russians take a suitably robust outlook. It is called "being offended," and it is an age-old Russian national pastime unifying forces at work in their vast nation—not only today, but during the seven decades of the Soviet era and back into the centuries of tsars and serfs. The Bratva and sestrinstvo - brotherhood of gangsters use it all the time."

"I know of it," says Chuck - what's the word now?

'obidet'sya,' which means 'to take offense,' and if you have ever worked with Russians, they have another word obidet,' which means 'to give offense.'

Fascinating as this is, I need more than help with my Russian verbs, " says Brophy, "I need an escape route."

"What's the trade?" asks Chuck bluntly.

"I'll give up the chain that I know about. Beyond Antonovich. It leads to somewhere interesting; I promise you."

"What, to Putin?" asks Chuck, "I could guess that much."

"No, the dots. You need to know which dots to follow and through which countries. Like Brant and Raven, but more than that. My price is that you will help me get lost."

"Can't do that," says Chuck, "your trade isn't enough. And your threat level has dwindled since you messed up with Salterton."

She looks around the pleasant drinking area where we are sat. Then she stands. "Okay, have it your way, but this isn't the last time you'll be seeing me."

There is a small popping sound, and the air is

suddenly filled with acrid red smoke.

I see Clare covering her face with her hand and wonder why Chuck seems unphased by what has just happened. Other guests are running for cover including some who appear to be running into the main indoor bar area.

The whole scene takes less than 90 seconds and yet Amelia has escaped. An electric bicycle parked against the railings was all she needed. She rode the bicycle along a short alleyway and then against the one-way traffic flow in this part of Dittlesham.

"Clever," says Chuck, "It's a domestic-use ring pull smoke grenade. They use them for parties. Or in this case, enough to intimidate but insufficient to incapacitate. She's sending us a signal. She can be far more deadly, but still sees us as her route to freedom."

"How do you know that?" asks Clare.

"She could have followed that with something altogether more deadly. Instead, she ran. She is telling us she really needs our help."

"But she is a killer!" says Clare, "Not someone we should mess with!"

"Agreed," answers Chuck, "Which is why she told us

she needs help and is prepared to negotiate. And she told us more as well. Did you notice she used sestrinstvo as well as bratva?"

"No, you lost me when you started talking about Russian verbs," said Clare.

Chuck explains, "Well - Bratva is like the fraternity of gangsters and the sestrinstvo implies a sisterhood. It means that Adam Antonovich is probably himself being run by a woman.

"Shmagina Alina Petrovna, " says Clare, "You must remember her? She arrived with Adam, - black silk dress, with fantasy leather boots? I was chatting to her for quite some time. She seemed to be well-connected and knowledgeable. Jake - you are giving me one of those looks."

I suppose I was. I remembered the decorative Alina, but that was how I'd placed her - accompaniment for Adam Antonovich - not as someone with a pivotal role. Yet now I was having to consider that she was running Adam and was probably well connected into the oligarchy.

The red smoke had cleared; we made light of it to the other guests. I realised that this was also a boating community, and that they were accustomed to smoke flares, admittedly usually on the water.

"Our friend is a practical joker. She got us good!" I notice the red dust from the smoke brushes easily from our clothes and faces.

"Er - did your friend leave this?" asks the server, holding a slim, black briefcase, with a new-looking scarf flamboyantly tied to its handle.. "She asked us to check it in to the wardrobe area, but I think she has forgotten it."

Chuck reaches out to take it, "We'll see it gets back to her - maybe we'll have the last laugh after all!"

The server smiles, "As long as it doesn't hold another smoke bomb!" she says, handing it to Chuck.

"Perhaps you are right, we'll open it later," Chuck says, smiling at the server. I look at the floor of our raised seating area. There's a red powder surrounding where the four of us have sat. I mentally calculate a large tip.

"Okay, the check, please, and could you call us a taxi to Magister Grange?" asks Chuck as we prepare for the return trip.

## *Sightseeing?*

We walk out of the seating area, and along the small alleyway through which Amelia escaped. A blue electric taxi is waiting there, silently pulled into the end of the alleyway so that traffic can get past on the one-way system.

Chuck motions by holding his finger across his mouth for both of us to be quiet in the car. We nod back. We don't want the taxi driver spreading stories to his passengers.

Then the ride back to Magister Grange. First we exit Dittlesham, past a small bookshop, a cheese shop and then a few twists down to the quayside, along next to a railway line, and turn right over a level crossing. Then more twisting roads that take us out of the 20-mph zone and back onto a two-way road towards Magister Grange. I think back to our earlier time on this road when we first arrived and of just how much has happened in between.

We only get as far as the steps of The Grange, when I can see Emmanuelle running towards us.

"Hold me," she whispers. As I do so, she hugs me and then presses some paper into my left jacket pocket. She breaks away and looks into my eyes. I can tell she has left me something important but doesn't want others to see.

Then I turn to see our now resident detectives, Penrose and Trewella, walking towards me.

"You're getting quite a welcome," states Trewella, looking over to Emmanuelle, "Where have you been in the taxi?"

"Sightseeing," I answer, "The river is beautiful, and I wanted to see more of it than we can from across the vineyards here. Show it to Chuck as well. It's quite different here from his home state in America. Then a quick look around Dittlesham: The pubs and the Quayside. We stopped for a quick drink in The Tribute but then made our way back here."

"I found a new scarf in one of the vintage shops," explains Clare, glancing at the scarf tied to the strap of Amelia's mystery briefcase.

"But no sign of Christopher Law?" asks DCI Penrose.

Chuck answers, "No, although we were not looking for him. I guess we could go to his room at the Drake Arms if we were really trying to find him."

"We have already visited there, but although he checked in, his room was empty and had been made up by the hotel cleaners. Nothing to see."

"What about Amelia Brophy?" asks Chuck," Has she turned up yet?"

Penrose answers, "No, although we found the RIB boat that she stole close near to Dawlish Warren. It's only a few minutes' walk from there to the train station and then 3 hours or so to London. We are waiting for her to use a card or make a call from there."

Amelia Brophy was right, the police had assumed she would bolt to London to evade capture.

"Well, we three all need to get inside to freshen up," says Clare, "Please excuse us."

With that, we walk into the still bustling hall of the Grange and head for our rooms.  I see Rishi briefly stop Clare, "Something you should know," he says, "See you in the Saloon, maybe around 5pm?"

*Open the briefcase*

Back at Magister Grange, we go back to my room. We have the briefcase but by now I'm reticent to open it in case it has been booby-trapped by Brophy.

Chuck takes a simpler view. "If Brophy had wanted to finish this, she could have done so when we were in that pub. No. I think she wanted us to take the case and it must somehow contain further evidence. That was quick thinking, Clare by the way, hiding it in plain sight in front of the detectives!"

He pulls at the clasps on the case and it pings open. There's no explosion, and the case seems to contain papers.

Chuck looks at both Clare and I.

"Things just got very dark," he says as he spreads the top document so that we can all read it.

*US PENTAGON - EYES ONLY*

TOP SECRET
Directed Energy Weapons

The United States needs to incorporate defense against directed energy weapons with the same intensity used developing anti-ballistic missile defenses. One of the major drawbacks to optical or directed energy systems is the inability to penetrate clouds or dense fog. Advances in technology are bringing weather phenomena under our control.

Increased computing power and micronized delivery systems will allow us to create specific perturbations in local atmospheric conditions. These perturbations allow for the immediate and lasting ability to create localized fog or stratus cloud formations shielding critical assets against attack from energy-based weapons.

Blending weather systems management using nanotechnology with UAVs and AI unmanned tanks will provide land and air supremacy in battlefield scenarios. This can have a direct read across into subsequent reparations work, creating an ideal positive loop for Brant Industries.

The future of nanotechnology will enable creation of stratus cloud formations to defeat DEW and optically targeted attacks on United States assets. The solution to the weather control problem involves networked miniature balloons feeding and receiving data from a four-dimensional variation (4d-Var) computer model through a sensor and actor network.

A network of diamond-walled balloons enters the area to be changed and then both measures and affects localized temperature and vapor content. This system effectively shortens the control loop of an atmospheric system to the point it can be "managed." The capabilities in the diamond-walled balloons are based on the future of nanotechnology.

*What we've just read*

"Wow," says Clare, "Are you sure this is in the public domain?"

"Er, it has TOP SECRET markings on it," says Chuck.

"Now I'm understanding the fog of war," I say.

"Yes, if the US Government is writing about weather manipulation, Unmanned Aerial Vehicles and AI Tanks, then it is like they have a whole new military system ready for deployment," observes Chuck, "Look, the paper goes on to talk about a mission."

"Weather Operation White Carpet," I read it out loud. "The strike package is a complex mixture of fourth and fifth generation aircraft, integrated with unmanned aerial vehicles (UAV). "

"This is describing offensive capabilities, rather than defence?" asks Clare.

Chuck nods, "The lead element into the area of regard (AOR) is a set of strike UAV's. - The name gives it away - As these unmanned aircraft enter the threat areas, the enemy integrated air defense system (IADS) becomes fully active."

"The ability to engage the strike package is limited to surface-to-air missiles (SAM) and anti-aircraft-artillery (AAA), " explains Chuck, drifting into military-speak.

"There we have it," says Clare, reading over Chuck's shoulder, "Sophisticated directed energy weapons (DEWs) attempt to engage but are thwarted by a cloud layer between the strike aircraft and the ground. The unmanned vehicles make short work of the surface systems, essentially following the guidance and infra-red (IR) signatures of the launch sites."

"This is scientific warfare by computer," I observe.

"Yes, it is very high technology. More than throwing missiles at one another," agrees Chuck.

I read some more, "The manned fighters and bombers enter the target area with a reduced threat array. After disposing of enemy fighters and avoiding or evading kinetic surface-to-air weapons, each aircraft delivers their deadly payload. The enemy is reliant upon DEW defense systems."

"But what are these DEW systems?" asks Clare.

"Directed Energy Weapons, like something from science fiction," explains Chuck. "There's a surprising amount of them around and they can fire at a target but leave no trace aside from target elimination."

"So what is it?" I ask, "Some kind of laser beam or ray gun?"

"Correct," says Chuck, "I remember when I was still working with missiles in Arizona, the DEWs were coming alongside fast.

"There's microwave weapons; The Active Denial System is a millimetre wave source that heats the water in a human target's skin and thus causes incapacitating pain - the US have experimented with it for crowd control. Then there's Vigilant Eagle which directs high-frequency microwaves towards any projectile that is fired at an aircraft. The system comprises a missile-detecting and tracking subsystem (MDT), a command-and-control system, and a scanning array."

Chuck looks around, "Now, have you heard of the BOFORS gun? It was used for anti-aircraft protection in the second World War, firing rapid, huge shells at planes. Developed by the Swedes, it was incredibly effective. Bofors still develop new weapons including the Bofors HPM (High Powered Microwave) Blackout which is said to destroy a wide variety of electronic equipment at short range.

Chuck continues, "And the list goes on, effective radiated power (ERP) of the Green Pine radar. It sends out signals like a Christmas tree with all of those pine needles.. Then there's active electronically scanned arrays (AESA) mounted on fighter aircraft as directed energy weapons against missiles. There's even an anti-drone rifle, which is a battery-powered electromagnetic pulse weapon. Both Russia and Ukraine used these during the Russian invasion of Ukraine.

Chuck pauses for breath, then continues, "Recently, an electric car maker discussed building a unique super tank with the idea triggered by the Russo-Ukrainian War.

"The tank design project is being implemented jointly with the German Defense Consortium. Germany's largest military conglomerate, Rheinmetall recently unveiled a concept fire support vehicle called the Lynx120, weighing 44 tons, which features Rheinmetall's 120mm smoothbore gun firing DM11 programmable high-explosive shells.

"Special protection modules enable mission-specific

responses to ballistic threats and improvised explosive devices. In addition, it is equipped with Rheinmetall active defense systems for the defense of rockets and anti-tank missiles."

"Wow," I say, "Add in laser weapons and it becomes formidable!"

"Add in laser, plus particle-beams, plasma and even sonics to get the full picture," observes Chuck, "And now there are rumours of a TRIGAX gun in space - Three beams which when they intersect are lethal."

I'm thinking of Ghostbusters, but I keep a straight face.

"Let's net this down," says Clare. "The report is describing a step change in warfare. Weather system control, Unmanned aircraft, Artificial Intelligence electric tanks and miscellaneous 'ray guns'. Scary stuff."

"Now you can see why Jago Fox was activated," Continues Chuck, "He was on to something big."

## *Emmanuelle's note*

I reach into my pocket, find the note from Emmanuelle, and read it.

*"I know.*

*Jago and I discussed how something like this could happen.*

*Many times.*

*And our escape route.*

*I trust you and Clare.*

*Emmanuelle xx."*

*What they do in the shadows*

"It's time to call Amanda," I say, "In say, Cold War times, there would be a risk of interception of our call. Now we can simply fire up a call through an encrypted social media channel to have the conversation."

"I agree, " said Chuck, "Things move along."

I call Amanda on my cellphone, using a well-known chat service. She picks up straight away.

"Hello, I guess you are still in Exeter and have news?" she asks, "Give me five minutes and I'll call you."

I hang up and tell the others what she has requested.

"She must be somewhere public and wants to get to a private location," assumes Chuck.

"So what will we tell her?" asks Clare, "I mean, we really want extra information from her."

She's right about us still being in Exeter. I'd expected to have left by mid-afternoon on Sunday, still nursing a hangover. Instead, I'm still here in Dittlesham and wondering whether there is a life outside Magister Grange.

Then, my phone rings. It is Amanda.

"I'm on speakerphone," she says, "There's someone else here."

A cough and then a voice.

"Jake, my old buddy. And Clare. Sorry to give both of you the run-around. Needs must, don't you know?"

It's Jago. I wonder why I'm not more surprised.

"And I assume that Chuck is with you?" asks Amanda.

"Yes, hello Jago, I'm a long-standing friend of Jake and Clare."

"And one who can be totally trusted," adds Clare.

"So Jago, I never had you marked out as a spy?" I ask.

"Think about it. Oxford. Politicians. Cambridge. Spies. It all makes sense, " says Jago, "Heck, even you, dear friend, are almost a spy. Amanda here tells me you've even been detained in this very facility!"

"True enough," I say, "But you seem to be firmly on the payroll."

"Yes, but it's not like James Bond, you know. I don't get unlimited expenses to swan off to Monaco and Patagonia."

"No, but I suppose it helps running a stately home in Devon?" says Clare, giggling.

"Come on then, let's hear it," says Clare, "The story so far and then we'll see what we can add."

"Well, you know my father created FST, the high-tech company that now makes the Ikiru chipset for electric cars? After he died, I inherited the company and have seen the demand increase enormously. Of course, there have been attempts to buy me out, but like my father before me, I've always resisted them.

"The latest is a bid by a Russian conglomerate, who I think are influenced by the Russian mafia. They are trying to weaponise the chipset so that it can be used in war machines, both tanks and aircraft."

"That's why we reactivated Jago," says Amanda, "So that he could dig further into the influencers driving the deal. We think it stretches a long way through the Kremlin."

"We'd worked out that Adam Antonovich must be the money source?" said Clare.

"Yes, you are kind of correct, " says Jago, "Except Antonovich is being run by someone else. By his sexy partner Shmagina Alina Petrovna. Alina has direct like to the Solntsevo.

"I'm lost now," I say, "What is Solntsevo?"

Amanda explains, "We are talking about high-ranking Moscow based mafia. Alina is high up in the Solntsevskaya and a sister-in-law to Vyacheslav 'Yaponchik' Ivansky the Russian mobster. Ivansky was a Pakhan - like a Mafia Godfather - and was brokering between two rival criminal groups before he was shot from 70 metres as he left a Thai restaurant. His killer fired from a car parked on the opposite side of a highway.

Jago continues, "Ivansky had a high-profile funeral, with flowers from various other mobster affiliated bratva (gangs) ."

"Yes," says Amanda, "But Ivansky had also done deals with the FSB. They knew Ivansky could organise the storage of the Russian mobster's obschak - that's their common fund of money. It's a really big deal to be given custodianship of that fund."

Jago adds, "But that's how the old vory-v-zakone ('thieves-in-law') system started to collapse. So much money was now in play via Ivansky's old empire and one-by-one the various players were toppled, with Alexei Petrov the successor to Ivansky."

I'm impressed. Jago used to skirt facts expertly. I wonder whether he's making this up, but it seems too consistent with what Amanda Miller is saying.

Amanda continues, "Petrov was slippery, with a variety of names and residences. Allegedly, he was involved in trafficking narcotics from Central and South America. Then, although Petrov tried to prevent the collapse of Ivansky's criminal empire, both Mikhas Solntsevskaya and the Semion Mogilevich crime network gained Ivansky's criminal assets. Then, Petrov was beaten and stabbed to death by two men in Zaporozhye, Ukraine.

Jago adds, "For much of this time, Alina was in the shadows. Never a clear front role, although gaining more power and money at every turn. It's a reason we are tracking this with such interest, because we believe it links back directly to the Kremlin."

"And we all know what that means..." says Clare.

## *Things we know*

"So what else do we know?" asks Clare,

"Who would have inherited Jago's business? I'm guessing at Christopher Law.

"And what part does Abigail Holbrook play in all of this? Let's suggest that she and Christopher were an item."

"What, not Jago?" I ask.

Jago replies, "No, never! Whenever I hear about my latest rumoured fling, I think how idle the minds must be that serve up the tittle-tattle. If I'd been with all the women I'm rumoured, then I'd need more moves than Mallanagana Vatsyayana."

"Mister Kama Sutra?" asks Clare.

"Are we getting off track?" asks Chuck.

Jago interrupts, "Abigail and Chris were close, but I always suspected Abigail of manipulating Chris like it was some kind of money play. Oh yes, and there was an innuendo in Magister that Abigail could supply drugs. It could explain some excesses I saw with some of our house guests."

"We've also received some intel from Amelia Brophy," I add, "She literally handed it to us."

"Amelia Brophy was the party organiser!" says Jago, "Abigail organised Amelia's contract to arrange the celebration."

"Well, she seemed to know about your bungling assassin, arranged by Adam Antonovich," explained Clare, "and was even given the job of cleaning up after him."

"Who, though?" asks Jago, "I was told it was Ian Salterton, who I can remember was something of a nuisance during the party."

Chuck answers, "Correct, but it looks as if he was a hired assassin too. Although it looks as if he was expecting to use a sniper rifle to take you down."

"It's lucky then, that I'd received the tip-off and could exit myself before he had a chance" answered Jago.

"But why so many confusing signs?" asked Clare, "We could not understand any of it."

Jago replies, "It was deliberate, to put everyone in a tail-spin. I couldn't even tell Emmanuelle what I was doing, except to say she should not believe anything that happened on Saturday but should play along with it. She did know about my other role though."

Chuck asks, "But where did you get your tip-off then?"

Jago answers, "It was Chris. He said I should be very careful because he'd picked up that someone was plotting against me. He emphasised it could end badly, but he didn't know the source. I assumed the worst, that someone had broken my cover. Chris didn't know about my deep role with the intelligence services. But Chris's tip-off meant I started to put together my escape plan. That was a good couple of weeks ago."

"But you'd told Emmanuelle?" I ask, thinking about her hastily concealed note.

Jago stutters, "Er, yes, I had to tell Emmanuelle something. Not the detail of what I was about to do, but enough that she wouldn't be completely distraught. I guess we can tell her more now the cat is out of the bag!"

"But what about the police?" asks Clare, "We can't keep this from Penrose and Trewella."

Amanda speaks with a steely tone to her voice, "No, you must keep it away from them. They should continue to act as they are now. Baffled at the mystery of Jago's death, surprised at the attempt on Ian Salterton's life and completely focussed on the drug ring."

"We should also tell you about something we received from Amelia Brophy,' said Clare, "It's quite disturbing. It looks as if the Americans are up to something. Something which the Russians intend to acquire."

"Operation White Carpet, I assume?" says Amanda.

"Yes, that's right," answers Clare.

"Operation White Carpet was part of a US Disinformation Campaign," says Amanda. "It was after the hacked US elections. I'm reading from a once confidential report to the US Senate."

"Can you do that?" asks Clare, surprised.

"Oh yes, this is now from the U.S. Government Publishing Office and the title is 'Disinformation'," answers Amanda., "Let me quote..."

"The U.S. intelligence community unanimously assessed that Russia sought to hijack the US democratic process, and specifically the presidential elections. Russia's strategy and tactics were not new, but their brazenness certainly was. We can understand how the Kremlin made effective use of its hacking skills to steal and weaponise information and engage in a coordinated effort to damage a particular candidate and to undermine public confidence in our democratic process.

"Of course, much of his is well-known, about how Russia deployed a deluge of disinformation in a broader attempt to undermine America's strength and leadership throughout the world."

Amanda paused and we could hear a page turn. Old school - she was reading from a paper copy.

"Russia's President, Vladimir Putin, ordered a deliberate campaign to undermine the US election. First Russia struck at political institutions by electronically breaking into the headquarters of one of the political parties and stealing vast amounts of information.

"Russian operatives also hacked emails to steal personal messages and other information from individuals ranging from Clinton Campaign Manager John Podesta to former Secretary of State

Colin Powell.

"This stolen information was then weaponised. We know that Russian intelligence used the Guccifer 2 persona and other mechanisms like WikiLeaks at seemingly choreographed times that would cause maximum damage to one candidate.

"This goes back to Hilary Clinton vs Donald Trump?" asks Clare.

"Correct," answers Chuck, "And most of this campaigning was carried on social media."

Amanda continues, "Russia did this with an unprecedented level of sophistication
about American presidential politics."

"They wanted to put the crooked one into power?" asks Clare.

"The controllable one, in thrall to the Kremlin," answers Chuck.

Amanda continues, "Second, Russia continually sought to diminish and undermine our trust in the American media by blurring our faith in what is true and what is not. Russian propaganda outlets like RT and Sputnik successfully produced and peddled disinformation to American audiences in pursuit of Moscow's preferred outcome. This Russian propaganda on steroids was designed to poison the national conversation in America."

"It seemed to drop an unfortunate choice of leader into the White House," muses Chuck.

Amanda continues, "The Russians employed thousands of paid internet trolls and botnets to push out disinformation and fake news at a high volume, focusing this material onto Twitter and Facebook feeds and flooding social media with misinformation. This fake news and disinformation was then hyped by the American media echo chamber and social media networks to reach and potentially influence millions of Americans."

"Incredible power of the social media, no wonder there have been fights about who can own it or control it," adds Clare.

I remember that it was Trump who used the phrase 'Fake News' the most. How ironic.

Amanda continues, "Russia continues these sorts of actions as we speak. Some of our close allies in Europe are experiencing exactly the same kind of interference in their political process. Germany has said that its parliament has been hacked. French presidential candidates have been the subject of Russian propaganda and disinformation. In The Netherlands the Dutch hand-counted their ballots because they feared Russian interference in their electoral process. Perhaps most critically for us, there is nothing to stop them from doing this all over again."

Amanda adds, "For instance, an individual associated with the Trump campaign accurately predicted the release of hacked emails weeks before it happened. This same individual also admits to being in contact with Guccifer 2, the Russian intelligence persona responsible for these cyber operations. There are many further examples."

"It explains the mysterious resignations by those close to power after that result," says Clare.

Amanda speaks, "Of course, the system worked both ways. As well as playing information into the US system, the Russians believed they were able to obtain information of strategic value as a result of their hacks. That is how artefacts such as Operation White Carpet - about a new computerised battlefield - were planted. They were strategically left in places likely to be intercepted as bait for the Kremlin."

"But how do you know so much about all of this?" asks Clare.

"It is where I come into the picture," says Jago, suddenly, "They needed to set a trap, to draw out the Russian players and look for the link back to the top. I was already set up as a sleeper agent. Some might see me as one in a high place too. My company FST could become the game in play, with an apparent opportunity to sell it, which is exactly where the Russians came along."

"I see, you'd sell FST to help the Russians, via Brant, make AI-based electric tanks?" I ask.

"Yes, but that isn't enough. The Russians need to believe that the Americans had a bigger game. A new managed battlefield with remote controlled planes, AI-electric tanks, and control of the weather systems," answers Jago.

"Except you weren't selling?" asks Clare.

"Deliberate," says Jago, "We needed to draw out the bigger players. Force the big chiefs to 'get out of bed'."

Nice. Quite a plan. Except the bit where Jago gets killed.

"Of course, when I got the tip-off that the Russians were on to me, I had to fake my own confusing death," explains Jago, "That way control passes to Christopher, who becomes the new owner. To tip the scales, if Abigail Holbrook also needed money, then it could help weaken Christopher's resolve about not selling the company."

Amanda adds, "We need to be clear about the opponents we're facing. Russia thinks nothing of throwing an elbow in the face, and routinely cheats to get its way. We've had success in getting some of their players disgraced and that is why we are chasing down the ringleader in this current situation. But of course, this isn't a game. Which is why it's so crucial that the UK grows its resilience. Alongside MI5's work with the police, SIS, and GCHQ amongst others to detect and disrupt threats we need a concerted response. It's how Jago has become reactivated and why it is so important that we apprehend the ringleaders."

She pauses, then adds, "In a way that disgraces them in the eyes of the Kremlin."

We'll need to think of something to get the money brokers of this clandestine takeover to really rile the Kremlin.

"Jago? Are you still on speakerphone?," asks Chuck.

"You bet. Now we must draw the main players into the open. That was my original mission, to find the links back to the Kremlin and the ways they were trying to change warfare."

"We'll have to decide who we can tell and who needs to remain in blissful ignorance," says Clare.

"Well, the cops should probably be left in the dark. Otherwise, it compromises their position," says Chuck.

Jago speaks, "We need Chris to re-appear, indicate he is prepared to sell, but that there are some conditions. He can disclose that a poison pill has been created in the Memorandum of FST."

"I see," says Amanda, "but that the clause can be removed within the right legal framework."

"What, with an additional payment, or something else?" asks Clare.

Jago answers, "My original plan. A stake in the acquirer - in this case Brant, to be negotiated right here in Magister Grange."

I decide that Jago has been hiding his talents and that he makes a great undercover agent.

"Once we have everyone here, we can run the second part of my plan," says Jago.

"What's that?" asks Clare.

"We leak that Ikiru doesn't actually work. The AI-based electric car trials have been faked with a second person driving the car remotely," answers

Jago.

"The best person to discover that would be Bettina. She would also be the most convincing person to tell the rest of the acquirer team," says Clare.

"But Brant and Zillian can't know any of this," says Chuck, "And if we are bringing in a lawyer, than I'd quite like to add a 'lawyer' of my own to the meeting."

"What specialism?" I ask.

"Oh, Ideally can speak Russian and knows how to handle firearms," says Chuck, "She is already on the way."

I realise he is referring to Christina Nott, who I had assumed was still in our London office.

*Bored stay-at-home parents*

We adjourned to the large dining area again. The local guests had, by now, mainly left Magister Grange, for their short journeys home. The Woodmantons, the Campbells, Blair Wight, Nat Retallick and Rose Marsh had all departed.

I noticed that Doctor Ellis had not returned, but also that the main staff of Magister Grange were all still present. Pascal Duret, Abigail Holbrook, and Margaret Mason, plus Faith, Maisy, Lily, and Zoe, along with Robin Duggan, the gardener.

I couldn't see the musicians, although it jolted my memory to find Rishi.

He was seated at a small table in the bar area of the Saloon, chatting to Jallie T. He stood as I approached and gestured for me to take a seat.

"Hi Jake," he says, "And Clare!"

"Hi, and where are your other musical compadres?" I ask.

"Alex Hayes - Drax - and his entourage have left. They have a gig in Bristol tonight. He's a busy lad," explains Rishi, "Josh wanted to get back to Vancouver. He caught a fast train from Exeter and then a link to Heathrow. A flight this evening and he'll be back home tomorrow."

A short pause and then he starts, "That wasn't why I wanted to see you. We think there's been some kind of drug dealer ring at Magister Grange."

Rishi says what we were beginning to suspect.

"For the concert of Saturday, my security team noticed the amount of dealing occurring. It wasn't like a regular gig with a few people making a little bit of extra MDMA money on the side."

Rishi continues, "To be clear - our whole crew are banned from any usage. But with all of our touring, we see the trends. Recreational weed isn't popular away from bored stay-at-home parents and the schoolyard. Compare the much better markup on MDMA, which is much easier to distribute and sell compared to smelly cheesy weed. And pills can be bought for £3 and sold for a tenner. As dealers said, as soon as you know what you're doing, it's easy. "

Jallie T speaks, "It's a shame that all gigs, football matches and other large groups of people attract dealers. The amount we have to spend on security. It's ridiculous."

I knew of this situation from my time working at Street magazine but had never delved into it. Rishi made it sound more like a day-to-day occupational hazard in rock music.

He continues, "But here at Magister Grange there's been a whole extra level running. Almost like wholesale. And it seemed to be cocaine cut with lidocaine (something like Denela). Lidocaine acts as an accelerant to cocaine. During the gig they were literally handling kilo lumps that looked as if they had been pressed into cubes with a car jack."

"But how much would that sell for?" asks Clare.

Jallie T answers, "It depends, London prices are higher, but down here in the West Country, it can be as little as £20,000 per kilo. But you have to remember that a kilo direct from Columbia can be as low as US$2,000."

Rishi grimaces, "And that's when I started to follow the line back. I could see that here were a lot of pointers all leading back to the same person. Abigail Holbrook."

"Abigail?" asks Clare.

I'm also thinking how this ties back to the Christopher Law conversation.

Rishi continues, "Rumour is that Abigail has great drug baron ambitions but had over-extended and gone into debt with her suppliers. She was trying to fund an import operation, and it all fell apart. Her entire stake in a shipment was impounded, and she took around a £200k hit."

"How do you know this?" I ask Rishi.

"The security around our gigs means we get a lot of random information. I just pieced some of it together. You might have heard about an arrest off Exmouth, when more than 200 kg of cocaine was seized. That's when Holbrook's plan started to unravel.

"A Cornish man and five Albanians were arrested on a luxury yacht and held on suspicion of drug trafficking. The group were sailing in a Jamaican-flagged vessel when they were intercepted off the coast, moving towards Exeter.

"The yacht was sailing from Antwerp and intercepted and boarded by specialist Border Force and National Crime Agency officers. It looked as if the drugs had been shipped from Columbia in a container which was then swapped for an EU-container in Antwerp. The consignment could then be offloaded without further customs checks and a part of it went into the yacht. Antwerp is notorious for drug trafficking."

"These drugs (including Abigail Holbrook's share) would have been sold on into communities across the UK by organised crime groups (OCG) purely motivated by money."

"So, Abigail Holbrook was trying to set herself up as a distributor?" asks Clare.

"Correct," answers Rishi, " We should ask those two policemen about this."

"It'll be next on the list," said Clare.

*A policeman's lot*

*When a felon's not engaged in his employment*
*Or maturing his felonious little plans*
*His capacity for innocent enjoyment*
*Is just as great as any honest man's*
*Our feelings we with difficulty smother*
*When constabulary duty's to be done*
*Ah, take one consideration with another*
*A policeman's lot is not a happy one*
*When constabulary duty's to be done, to be done*
*A policeman's lot is not a happy one, happy one*

*Gilbert and Sullivan*

## *Class A Problem*

We made an appointment (an appointment!) to see DCI Penrose and DI Trewella. I guess it was their attempt to introduce a power structure.

We showed up at the ad-hoc office of the police at the correct time and a constable (a different one) showed us into their centre of operations.

"Hello," said Clare, "We've invited Chuck Manners along this time. You'll know he attempted to chase the sniper until she escaped across the River Exe."

"Yes, hello to you all, Mr Lambers, Ms Crafts said you have some new information for us?"

"That's right," I say, "About drugs."

I notice Trewella shift uneasily, and I think we are onto something.

"We know about the drug ring," says Penrose, "It was the reason we were originally monitoring Magister Grange."

"I wish you'd said something, it would have saved us quite a lot of time," I say.

"Well, since we are amongst Crown Operatives here, I guess I can say more," answers Penrose.

I see her look across toward Trewella.

"We had a tip off which let us apprehend a dealer Chaka Noon, who ran a county lines operation around this area and boasted about her lavish lifestyle. It was funded by selling Class A on Snapchat. She was from Birmingham but sold the drugs 180 miles away. It was a classic county lines setup.

"She took pictures inside her BMW car while also posting photos of bundles of cash on social media.

"Was she mad?" asked Clare, "Why not make it easy to get caught?"

Trewella continues, "Ms Noon's elaborate 25-year - old lifestyle came crashing down when she was pulled over while driving down the M5 after our tipoff. Noon had been travelling from her home in Birmingham in a blue BMW to Exeter when officers from Avon and Somerset police stopped her near Junction 22, south of Bristol."

Trewella continues, "I was on the case. She panicked as officers descended on her at which point she was seen throwing an object from the vehicle. Although never recovered, it is believed that she was disposing of Class A drugs. In her vehicle, police found a damaged mobile phone wedged between the seats in an attempt to destroy evidence. The phone's sim was still intact and was tracked as the relevant mobile involved in a certain county line operation. There was another phone with incriminating evidence found in her bedroom in Birmingham."

"I got involved in questioning her," said Trewella, "It was when we found out about Magister Grange. She told us that her main supplier in Devon was from a stately home east of Exeter."

"But did you know who the ringleader was here?" I ask.

"No, but it is why we had the Grange under surveillance," answers Penrose, "We even inserted an undercover operative here, because the stakes were so high - in the millions."

"Was it Zoe Demelza? As undercover? " asks Clare, "Only she seemed very clued-in for a student and domestic help."

"You are very shrewd," said Penrose.

"We should call her in. She may add something," suggests Chuck.

DCI Penrose reaches for her phone, ordering coffees and asks that Zoe bring them.

## *Camouflage*

There is a knock on the door and Zoe enters, pushing a trolley of coffees and cookies.

"Win-win for you," she says, "You get me and refreshments. At least my cover isn't blown outside of this room."

"I take it the trolley is camouflage?" asks Chuck.

"Yes, although there seem to be many people who have rumbled me now."

We explain to Zoe what we had discovered. She listens intently, then says, "I'd been working my way around trying to find out more about the drug ring. I didn't think it was anything to do with Jago and Emmanuelle. I guess Jago's death proves that point, although I still think there is something suspicious about the whole thing."

I remember Zoe didn't know about Jago being in London, and none of the others were saying anything.

"I wondered if it could be someone on the staff as a ringleader, but then I was close to the other staff, so I think someone would have let something slip. But nothing.

"I wondered whether the gardener, Robin Duggan, knew anything, so I attempted to get close to him, but again, nothing.

"Then there was Christopher Law. He had a reputation as a wild one, which would fit, but that drew a short straw, too. Although, something I didn't tell Clare was when I was trapped close together with Chris in that doorway was that he appeared to be frisking me."

"Are you sure?" I ask.

"Trust me, I can tell the difference," answers Zoe. I catch Clare looking at me with a 'how could you?' expression on her face.

Zoe continues, "There was the cook - Mrs Mason - and Dr Ellis, both of whom I quickly ruled out - in fact I suspected Dr Ellis was another person operating undercover - He had some of the moves. In terms of permanent people, it meant the remaining list was Pascal Duret and Abigail Holbrook.

"So is our prime suspect still Abigail Holbrook?" asks Chuck, "Think about it. She's allegedly running a low-end drug operation, but then invests a large sum in a fortune-changing wholesale shipment. The deal goes wrong, and she is left with no produce and no money. Now she is under the heat from her upstream suppliers."

Clare adds, "Abigail does the only thing she can think of and tries to get Christopher Law to fund her. The only thing is, Christopher could only get money from the sale of Jago's company."

Chuck says, "Except Jago didn't want to sell the company."

"And it sounds as if Christopher didn't want to support Abigail, judging by their argument the other day," I say.

I look at the expressions on the faces of the two police. They are both looking surprised at the revelations and how they fit together.

"Think about it. Leverage, " says Clare, "Someone wants Jago to sell his company, FST. He won't do it, but maybe his step-son will if the right pressure is applied. The buyers set a kill contract on Jago, which would leave Chris to inherit the company, so long as it happens before Jago marries Emmanuelle."

"Are you sure you are not both undercover agents?" asks DCI Penrose.

"It's what we do, but we are not under contract to anyone at this time," answers Clare, "We simply came down here to celebrate Jago and Emmanuelle's engagement."

"There are still a lot of moving parts," says Zoe, "I can't see that this is over."

That's about when we split to go back to our rooms. I can see the police are looking dumbfounded with the latest information, but I don't want to get tricked into revealing anything else.

We say our goodbyes and, as nonchalantly as possible, leave the police to their own discussions.

Chuck waves us towards the bar in Magister Hall. He includes Zoe in his gesture, but also suggests we should call Emmanuelle and invite her along.

"We need to get on the level with Emmanuelle now, " says Chuck.

Clare continues, "I will call Emmanuelle in a moment, but first think about it. Chris gets an inkling what could happen when Abigail approaches him for a loan of a monstrous £200k. Chris senses that something is wrong, refuses to help (as Jake heard in that garden argument) and tips off Jago that someone is gunning for him.

"Jago thinks his cover is blown and stages his own death, so that he can be safely relocated with Emmanuelle."

"We've still got Alina Petrovna to consider, " says Chuck, "linked to Adam Antonovich, and she is high in the Solntsevskaya, with its direct links to the Kremlin."

"That's it! " says Chuck, "The Kremlin are trying to force the outcome. They want the battlefield technology and are attempting to get it via Brant Industries."

"But Brant is American?" asked Clare, "Isn't it?"

Chuck answers, "Maybe, superficially, but it could be owned by oligarchs. Perhaps an agent of the Kremlin? Give them the technology and they can wage a better war. And conduct better clean-up operations afterwards. Its a despicable way to make a living, but they won't be the first."

"So what are you going to do?" asks Zoe, "We may have figured some of it out, but we can't leave it like this."

"We need a plan," says Chuck.

# PART THREE

## *Emmanuelle*

*Mélodie d'amour chantait le cœur d'Emmanuelle*
*Qui bat cœur à corps perdu*
*Mélodie d'amour chantait le corps d'Emmanuelle*
*Qui vit corps à cœur déçu*

*Tu es encore*
*Presque une enfant*
*Tu n'as connu*
*Qu'un seul amant*
*Mais à vingt ans*
*Pour rester sage*
*L'amour étant*
*Trop long voyage*

*Mélodie d'amour chantait le cœur d'Emmanuelle*
*Qui bat cœur à corps perdu*
*Mélodie d'amour chantait le corps d'Emmanuelle*
*Qui vit corps à cœur déçu*

*L'amour à cœur*
*Tu l'as rêvé*
*L'amour à corps*
*Tu l'as trouvé*
*Tu es en somme*
*Devant les hommes*

*Comme un soupir*
*Sur leur désir*

*Tu es si belle*
*Emmanuelle*
*Cherche le cœur*
*Trouve les pleurs*
*Cherche toujours*
*Cherche plus loin*
*Viendra l'amour*
*Sur ton chemin*

*Mélodie d'amour chantait le cœur d'Emmanuelle*
*Qui bat cœur à corps perdu*
*Mélodie d'amour chantait le corps d'Emmanuelle*
*Qui vit corps à cœur déçu.*

*Pierre Bachelet*

## *Close-fitting*

Clare and I meet Emmanuelle in the Green Drawing Room.

She arrives promptly and is in a close fitting mid-brown wool tweed country suit, with an elegant muted purple scarf around her neck, hair pulled back from her face.

"Oooh, hot!" says Clare, echoing my thoughts.

"It's Ralph Lauren," she whispers, "but looks like close-fitting Purdey."

"You can do the countryside vibe when it suits you," observes Clare.

Emmanuelle remains standing, "I guess you want to talk to me about Jago? I need to know..."

She trails off.

"He's still alive," says Clare, looking into Emmanuelle's eyes.

We both saw Emmanuelle tremble a little. "I knew it," she says, "I suppose he's in New York or somewhere by now?"

"London," answers Clare, "And very safe."

"Can I see him?" asks Emmanuelle, recovering her composure.

"How did you know?" asks Clare.

"He told me some of it. You know Jago. He said he was working for MI5. Thought of himself as a gentleman spy. I used to joke about him being a civil servant," she pauses.

"He never thought of it as dangerous. I did worry, though."

Then, she turn to me, "Jake, Did you know about it? About Jago and MI5?"

"Nothing, I swear. I'm still coming to terms with it now."

Emmanuelle picks up the thread again, "He told me a long time ago about his basic work. He regarded it as a side-line, which helped with some of his running expenses. No-one ever suspected, not the staff, his friends, no-one."

She sits down in on a chaise lounge. "Then he was asked to help set up some kind of deal. They needed to use the company - you know - FST to make it work. I became worried, but Jago said it was okay and that it would never amount to anything because of the safeguards he had put in place."

"Were those the financial safeguards?" I ask.

"Yes, plus the Will which moves everything to Christopher and me. Jago clarified that we should never sell out to a foreign state run organisation. He'd done something to sabotage the company. Something to do with the shares. Christopher knows all about it. Look, let me arrange for some coffee in here."

She reaches into her jacket and produces a slim telephone. "Hello Mrs Mason, could you arrange for some coffees to be brought around to the Green Drawing Room? Please ask Zoe Demelza to bring them."

Clare and I look at one another.

"Any special reason it's Zoe you've asked?" asks Clare.

"You must know by now that Zoe was someone from Jago's work? He knew that there was something else going on here. That Abigail was trying to start a drug ring. Zoe was instructed to stay undercover but collect more evidence."

"So Jago knew what Abigail was up to?" asks Clare.

"We didn't know whether it had anything to do with whatever else was going on here, so Jago asked for an investigation."

"So you knew about Zoe all along?" I ask.

"Yes, frankly, I'm amazed that the police didn't know about her when they descended upon Magister Grange."

"But what about Jago's apparent suicide?" I ask.

"He had prepared me for something big to happen during the weekend. He'd told me he thought he was now in danger and needed an escape route. He told me not to be too concerned but that strange games would play out over this event."

"That's how you kept your composure," said Clare.

"It is although I lost it several times," said Emmanuelle. She pauses again.

"...Like the time when we had to go upstairs with the doctor to identify Jago. The doctor had pronounced him dead, but I was sure I could still see him breathing. They would not let me touch him, and they only let us in for less than a minute."

She pauses again, as if thinking over the encounter.

"Oh, and that doctor. Dr Ellis wasn't it? I'd never seen him before and yet he seemed to be an invited guest to the whole event. I was immediately suspicious when he seemed to take control. I guess it was to prevent anyone from finding out the truth."

"That Jago had staged the whole thing?" said Clare, "I've got to say it all looked convincing to me when I went upstairs, but I suppose I should have realised that the dim lighting in the room was to help cover up the staging?"

I agree, "Yes, and then that quick getaway. Don't leave anyone time to look around. It really was like the Juliet scene from Shakespeare."

"It was better that I didn't know too much of Jago's plans, though. I still had people talking about me behind my back - like about the show must go on - and was I in it to grab Jago's fortune. It helped me to know who my true friends were. That includes both of you, of course!"

All three of us smile and Clare says, "It's time for a group hug."

## *En Vogue*

"So how are we going to end this?" Asks Emmanuelle.

"There's two major situations," answers Clare.

"First there's the one of the drug ring and Christopher's need to get funding to help Abigail. We've talked to Chris, and he knows about all of this and is entirely against it."

Clare pauses, then begins again, "We've also got the sale of FST to Antonovich, who we now think is being operated by Alina Petrovna."

"What she of the soft fantasy outfits?" asks Emmanuelle.

"She's been on the cover of Vogue, you know," answers Clare, "Emmanuelle, you were right to say that the deal has been sabotaged. There's some kind of 'poison pill' thing to do with the shares and also, it turns out that the Ikiru technology was faked, to make it seem more attractive."

"But why would Antonovich be in such a hurry to cut a deal?" asks Emmanuelle, "Surely it can happen at another time?"

"Not if they think that the Chinese are also pursuing it," explains Clare. "Antonovich is to be given a recording of a Chinese negotiation for FST. It's provided by Ian Salterton, who wants to get back into Antonovich's good books."

Emmanuelle asks, "But I thought Salterton was a hired assassin, after Jago?"

Clare smiles, "He was, but when he bungled everything, Antonovich took a dislike to him."

"Does anyone like Ian Salterton?" I ask.

There is silence.

## *Apache AH64E*

Monday morning and I decide to take some fresh air outside. There's still a great view across the River Exe and I'm struck by the tranquillity of the surroundings. Then, the other side of the vineyard, there is a small commotion. It's a louder noise than the occasional trains along either bank of the river, or of the take-offs from Exeter airport.

I look up and see a sleek green military helicopter on the last stage of its landing approach. I can't help but wonder if Christina is in it. It is certainly her style of arrival.

I don't have long to wait for an answer, my phone rings and I hear her voice.

"Hey Jake, I guess you've just seen me arrive? Where are you? Let's meet and get Clare and Chuck as well."

"Hey, I'm outside the house. There's a balcony with chairs and a great view out across the vineyard and down to the water. But I'll come back to the main entrance."

Sure enough, I see Christina, alone and carrying a long, round bag of the type one takes onto a yacht. She waves when she sees me, drops the bag, and runs across for a greeting.

"This is one cool place," she says.

She is dressed in blue camo combat fatigues, which could also look right in a bar in Camden.

"That was one cool entrance too! I think you win."

"What in that little old thing? Only an Apache AH64E! The latest British military helicopter. I asked the pilot if I could have a go, but he was really quite nervous about anyone else flying it."

I was reminded instantly of Christina's double life as a pop star and a Russian-trained agent who can fly planes, helicopters and operate munitions. Things are moving fast. I show Christina to my room in the Grange, where Chuck and Clare are already waiting, thanks to Clare's access key. They already have a phone line open to Amanda Miller back in London.

Clare explains the situation to Christina. Chuck adds the detail of his expectations of his new 'lawyer'. Amanda remains quiet.

Christina summarises, "Okay, I see. The Russians want to use Brant to acquire some war technology called Ikiru. We say no and have two financial impediments to prevent them. A poison pill which makes the deal worthless and secret knowledge that the technology they want to buy doesn't work.

"They want to bring in their chiefs to renegotiate the removal of the poison pill but they don't know Ikiru doesn't work.

"The main negotiators are connected to the top tier of Putin's inner circle. I guess they all know Bortnikov, Patrushev, Shoigu and Gerasimov, at least. Then with Alina Petrovna we are talking about high-ranking Moscow Solntsevskaya mafia.

"Jago Fox was the owner of FST, but everyone thinks he's been killed and his step-son Chris Law is to negotiate. The Russians think they have Chris caught in a honey trap with Abigail Holbrook because of her need to dig herself out of a failed drug deal.

"Oh, and I'm supposed to be one of the lawyers. Have I missed anything?"

I smile. Christina has summarised perfectly. I wonder what would happen if she were to ask our friends, the police, what was happening.

Now Amanda speaks, "Alina Petrovna's Solntsevskaya mafia has other high-ranking members. The ultimate leader nowadays is Colonel General Omurazat 'Strelli' Kovarin.

"Kovarin?" says Chuck, "I remember him. A war criminal who used air-dropped dart-like fléchettes in the Ukraine conflict against civilians. He used the same tactic to run enforcement in his patch in Moscow, but with fléchettes fired from Anti-tank weapons against his enemies.

Christina nods, "Yes, his nickname Strelli is short for Strelochka (стрелочка) - which means arrow. He allowed illegal weapons containing these dart-like unguided projectiles with a tiny tail fin to make them fly true.

"These tiny weapons were designed to be dropped from an aircraft or later combined into a warhead. They contain no explosive charge but as they fall they develop significant energy able to penetrate soft cover such as jungle canopy, several inches of sand or light armour. They do not leave unexploded ordnance (UXO) which could be active years after a conflict ended."

"But they left gruesome evidence of their deadly metal rain," adds Christina, "Kovarin authorised these weapons in Ukraine and as a result Putin bumped him up to his top table and let him run his Moscow bratva gangster ring on the side."

"Okay, it's decided," says Chuck. "We need to bring Kovarin over for the negotiation. Capture him and we've disabled a major gangster ring and brought in one of Putin's chief warmongers. Jago's undercover mission will have been successful beyond his wildest dreams."

"Luck is on our side," interrupts Amanda, "Kovarin is in London at the moment. His mistress Anastasia Vaskuvicha has been seen taking lunch in the Tiffany Blue Box cafe. Our agents had the most enormous expenses bill from that piece of surveillance."

Chuck asks, "Well, what do we think Kovarin was doing?"

"His laundry, we suspect," says Amanda, "He was meeting with a football club and then with a couple of investment banks."

"I see," says Christina, "Moving his dirty money into cleaner places,"

"Well, we need a reason to accelerate Kovarin's appearance in this deal," says Chuck

"How about a hint of China?" suggests Christina, eyes twinkling.

Now Amanda speaks, "The activities of the Chinese Communist Party pose the most game-changing strategic challenge. If China was interested in what FST are doing, it could be an added incentive for Russia to act fast."

She adds, "Russia can see the Chinese authorities playing the long game in cultivating contacts to manipulate opinion in China's favour - seeking to co-opt and influence not just prominent Parliamentarians from across the political landscape, but people much earlier in their careers in public life, gradually building a debt of obligation."

Clever. Use China to prod Russia's big chiefs to break cover.

Amanda adds, "The Chinese authorities use all the means at their disposal to monitor and intimidate the Chinese diaspora. This takes place all over the world, from coercing and forcibly repatriating Chinese nationals to harassment and assault."

I can see what Amanda is doing: She is using a State

threat which has already been identified by Russia. The Kremlin won't want China to get access to any of these new warfare systems, nor the intellectual property. It is a way to bait the hook.

Amanda speaks, "Russia already knows the Chinese authorities present a different order of challenge. They're trying to re-write the rulebook, to buy out everyone, and to recruit staff to work for them. It should be enough to bring an urgent response from Alina Petrovna and Strelli Kovarin. We just need to think about how best to seed this."

"Seed it through Adam Antonovich, " says Clare, "It will seem as if we have suspected none of this. But someone - probably Christopher - can tell Antonovich that there's been a second show of interest from China."

"Even better if there is some evidence of the transaction," says Chuck.

Clare speaks, "Use Ian Salterton, he can pretend that after his bungling, he is bargaining his way back into Antonovich's good books. He could have evidence that Christopher is starting negotiations."

"We can help with that," says Amanda, "We can manufacture a recording of Chris in a Zoom call with Beijing. Salterton can say he got access because of his contacts."

A plan is forming.

Although the scorpion's tail is used as an extremity for hunting, defense, and digging, it is not a modified leg or arm, but an entire body section that has evolved in favour of high mobility.

Scorpions have been extremely successful with this strategy for over 400 million years. Rather than being an appendage, the scorpion tail is composed of body segments. It contains muscles and nerves, as do limbs. There are five segments, with the notorious sting.

Functionally, the joint of scorpion tail resembles a hinge joint with two contact surfaces, as one would find in an arthropod leg. Unlike the hinge joint, however, the joint of the scorpion tail has no socket and no joint head, but two saddle-like structures that slide on an almost circular opening.

The principle, which is based on further structural peculiarities, allows the one-dimensional movement of a hinge joint to be extended by the possibility of twisting.

This study not only provides the first description of an arachnid body part, but it also suggests new designs for "soft robotics."

*Across the River*

There are still residual guests from the weekend in Magister Grange. They are staying on to visit the trade show in Exeter. I suspect it is to enjoy the complementary helicopter rides.

Clare decides to have an impromptu pub session and asks Emmanuelle where would be a good location.

"Across the River" suggests Emmanuelle, "We can go to the Pumping Station, It's an old pub on the route of one of Brunel's railways, except it was from the days when the railways ran on vacuum pressure."

I'd heard of this and could just make out the shape of the old station, with its tall tower, near to the shoreline of the River Exe.

"We can get a boat to take us across, and the pub has

a large tent in its garden where we could probably arrange a private party."

"It sounds like a brilliant idea," I say.

Emmanuelle speaks, "Yes, but don't be deceived by the distance. We have to go in a kind of arc to get there because of the tides and the sand banks."

"It will be a great opportunity to feed in the story about the negotiation," says Christina.

"Right, that's settled," says Clare.

***

Tuesday afternoon and we assemble for the river trip to the pub, having walked down the same grassy slope that earlier led Amelia Brophy to the high-powered RIB on which she escaped.

Some of the group had ducked out of this little soiree, including Adam Antonovich and Hubert Tempelmann. Christopher Law would also be available in Magister Grange today, ostensibly to talk to the police.

No great surprise that Ian Salterton was along on the ship - we'd insisted he play his part and Bianca and Clare would play theirs too.

I'm surprised to see a large colourful craft arrive to ferry us, and am told it is one of the boats that normally ferries people for bird spotting cruises and to look at the nearby Jurassic coastline and even along the canal back into Exeter. The skipper is used to all of the mysteries of what, to me, looks like a fairly flat and calm piece of water.

Then he points to a couple of landmarks.

"Those are a couple of yachts that sank here," he explains, "The owners couldn't afford the cost of recovery."

We are all aboard and I realise the boat is big enough to have two passenger decks and includes a bar and an area serving hot pasties. Of course, we are in the west country.

Underway and our influence strategy begins. Amanda had forwarded to Salterton a fake recording of a conversation between Christopher Fox and what was supposed to be the Chinese. They were suggesting a meeting the following week to finalise a deal which would transfer FST into their hands.

Amanda had provided the recording to Ian Salterton back in Magister Grange and he now had it on his phone. Salterton was now decidedly under the control of Amanda Miller and MI5, in order to escape a lengthy internment or worse. He was now earnestly telling Lawrence Booth that the Chinese were also negotiating, in the expectation that Lawrence would tip off Adam Antonovich. I could already see Lawrence on his phone, making an agitated call to someone.

It gave Adam Antonovich a couple of days to call up the Russian chiefs to respond if they wished to retain control. Meanwhile we'd also primed Bettina Kübler. It had to be plausible. She needed to know that the Ikiru self-driving artificial intelligence was being augmented by human drivers. We'd set up a conversation between Bianca and Clare in the ship's bar area, close to where Bettina was standing.

Bianca was telling Clare she was tired of Lawrence Booth, but no one seemed surprised. Bianca explained how she had met another man and it turned out he was ex-Formula One and now a driver for Zillian. Bettina was quietly listening to what could become a raunchy tale.

"Those formula one drivers are so - em - lean," said Clare.

"Tell me about it, " said Bianca, "But this one had a very unusual job driving fast cars around."

She told Clare that he'd explained to her that he was doing 'stealth driving' now for the new Ikiru-based cars. These cars were not clever enough to drive themselves and he had to sit flat in the cars and use a monitor screen to drive them around the tracks and even on the highway. He said it was like a slowed-down Xbox Formula One experience. Clare could see that Bettina was taking it all in. That the Ikiru system was not even half ready. It made a massive detrimental impact to the valuation of FST.

Now, Clare calls over Emmanuelle.

"What's this I hear about a Chinese delegation arriving this weekend? I'm told we need to be on our way by then?"

Emmanuelle smiles, "You can stay at mine if you need to, " she said, "Between you and me, Christopher has multiple options for the FST sale."

I could see Bettina's eyes nearly pop from her head at this news. Second source confirmation of the story that Lawrence Booth would bring back from Ian Salterton.

In parallel with all of this, Christopher Fox was deployed back at Magister Grange. He would ask about the plans of Antonovich and Tempelmann and suggest that they would need to have left before the weekend.

Later, on our way back to Magister Grange,

Christopher phones me.

"I talked to Antonovich the way we discussed. He made one request. To be honest, he sounded a little desperate. He wants to make an improved offer, using his chief negotiator. He proposed that Colonel General Kovarin visits Magister Grange on Thursday and, as he puts it, we finalise things. He explained that Kovarin has links to the very top of the Russian system."

"That's great," I'm thinking when he adds:

"I looked back at Antonovich. I could see him glance toward Alina Petrovna and notice her ever-so-slightly nod her head in agreement. Yes, Petrovna was the real source of power."

"Are you sure? I ask."

"Oh yes, I can't mistake that look."

*Kovarin*

Thursday morning and we are primed for the visit of Colonel General Kovarin. A ruthless gangster who also has control of significant actions of the Russian military.

My room's view was across the lawns and down toward the vineyard, beyond which was the River Exe. The soundproofing was good, because we had seen a succession of guests being ferried by helicopter to the conference in Exeter. It made me realise there was good money in car manufacture, or at least in its associated Public Relations.

Chuck, Clare, Christina, and I had assembled to watch the unfolding scene.

We recognised the two regular helicopters: a sleek white one and a slightly larger and more angular looking one. They were the main shuttle service to and from Exeter. Yet, from my room they could not be heard.

To one side was the aggressive looking green craft that Christina arrived in. Unmistakably a warplane, Christina had told me it could fly at over 200mph.

Nothing prepared me for the new helicopter carrying the Russians. White, with blue detailing, it looked enormous, even next to the Apache. It could carry 8 VIP passengers and arrived flanked by two smaller and apparently armed military helicopters. The main helicopter reminded me of something from a child's colouring-in book - 'H is for Helicopter'.

Chuck carried digital binoculars to study the passengers. I'd already asked Chuck about the military accompaniments and he explained that the three 'copters were all registered as Turkish, instead of Russian. "Using Turkey to bypass western sanctions," he explained.

I could see the people unload from the helicopter, including the man who I assumed was at the centre of the negotiation. He was escorted by another gazelle-like blonde woman, dressed to the nines in a creme and gold outfit, which I guessed was from her recent expedition to Kensington. They were surrounded by several chunky central casting types who I assumed were security.

"Game On," whispers Chuck, studying the disembarkation of military types from the other two helicopters, "These other men are Spetsnaz - and they look as if they are Alpha Group, by those shoulder patches."

It didn't mean anything to me, but Christina chipped in, "They will have been pulled from Ukraine if they are really Alpha Group. I can see the winged sword, and the Black cross with an 'A' - they look like Alpha directorate to me."

"It's significant if Kovarin has managed to get a unit of Alpha Group to accompany this so-called private sector mission. We are holding a scorpion by its tail."

*Aurora*

*Goddess sparkle*
*A mountain shade suggests your shape*

*I tumble down on my knees*
*Fill my mouth with snow*
*The way it melts*
*I wish to melt into you*

*Björk Guðmundsdóttir*

*Side bar and extreme force*

We had told DCI Penrose and DI Trewella about our new guests. We'd also explained that they had nothing directly to do with the drug smuggling. The two of them seemed satisfied and thought that there would be no trouble from a group having a confidential business meeting in one of the larger rooms in Magister House.

"We just don't want them coming into our police operation," explains DI Trewella, "It would be unfortunate if they saw what we have prepared in our investigation room."

They seemed so unaware of what was about to go down.

I had pieced together that Abigail Holbrook was short of cash was because the visiting Russians had leaked details of her smuggling operation. Also that it was only a side-bar to their main objective: To get

Ms Holbrook to persuade Christopher Law to sell his father's company.

Now we had a full-blown negotiation taking place in the well-protected Grand Saloon of Magister Hall. It was a huge State Room, flanked with three smaller rooms. The walls were hung with outstanding Venetian Giovanni Antonio Pellegrini murals. Emmanuelle had already described this room as sometimes used for magical weddings, but she was uncertain about using it for her own because she had seen so many prior ceremonies conducted there that it wouldn't feel unique.

I could see how it would be used to good effect for the Russian negotiations and the dominant fireplace and its accompanying impressive paintings would make a stunning backdrop for the chief negotiator. I was particularly struck by a painting of Aurora, goddess of the dawn, and wondered if the symbolism of the new dawn triumphing over Morpheus would be in any way emblematic.

True to form, Colonel General Kovarin's security detail moved in and made a thorough sweep of the Grand Saloon, looking for transmitters and other forms of espionage. They didn't find anything, except a Fitbit step counter which Chuck had previously placed on the floor as a test of the Russian security effectiveness.

Unknown to the security detail, Chuck had also been talking to Pascal Duret and Margaret Mason about the two-metre-wide secret passage which ran for ten metres along a side wall in the Grand Saloon and then to the open air by the side of a coal cellar.

I noticed that Adam Antonov and Alina Petrovna had been assisting the security operation and it was now abundantly clear that Alina was in the driving seat. No wonder Kovarin had her as a first-line officer in his bratva gang.

The meeting had been set for midday, and I realise the setup time had been kept short as a defence against security traps being sprung. Kovarin wanted the surprise element coupled with his intentional show of extreme force.

## *Negotiate*

The start of negotiations was set for 12:00 midday.

The room had received a makeover. It is now set out like one of Vladimir Putin's conferences, with a long table, at one end of which sat Kovarin. At the other end, some three metres away sat Christopher Law. Adam Antonov, Alina Petrovna, and her legal and security people were sitting along one long side of the table, with Christina, Chuck, and me among those on the opposite side.

I felt uncomfortable that there were yet more from the three helicopters sat behind me, including, worryingly, a couple of paramedics. We seem to be decidedly outnumbered.

Noticeably absent from the room were Bettina Kübler and Hubert Tempelmann. Maybe I'd misread the previous huddles of people after all?

Kovarin spoke good English with a low rasp, "I'll say this once only. Mr Law, I have been allowed to purchase your company for the price written on this piece of paper. To achieve such a high price, I have been authorised to use direct funds from the obschak which is currently under my custodianship."

This was unusual. Kovarin was being given direct access not only to Russian elite fighting units, but also to Russian gangster money. Operating like a mini-Putin.

Christopher is handed the paper by one of the suited men close to Kovarin, who has to stand and walk around the table to deliver it.

Christopher looks at the paper. I could tell from Chris's expression that the amount must have been exceedingly large. I remember Chuck's advice 'If it looks too good to be true, it probably is too good to be true.'

"If I accept this, it will be final and binding to both parties?" asks Christopher Law, keeping up the pretence that he was considering accepting the deal.

"Da," says Kovarin.

I can see another suited man close to Alina, frantically typing into a laptop. I do not know what he is doing. Then his phone rings and he answers it. He stands and looks at Alina Petrovna who shouts, *"Osadit' Kovarin! On nakhoditsya pod arestom!"*

"She just asked them to seize and arrest Kovarin," whispers Christina into my ear.

There are several metallic clicks and I sense that the room is now full of live armed soldiers. Some of those clicks came from behind me. It looks as if Alina is in control. It's another rung further up the ladder for her if she takes over from Kovarin.

Alina reaches under her jacket. Brings out a yellow intercom. Except it's not an intercom. It's a taser. She fires it at Kovarin. Two brightly coloured wires snake along the table where we are sitting. The barbs hit his lower neck, which I realise is above his Kevlar vest. Impact and a soft moan from Kovarin, who slumps forward onto the table. I can taste the electricity in the air. Like after a thunderstorm.

I think of the irony of Kovarin being shot by two barbs, not unlike the fléchettes upon which he built his terrible reputation. I notice his immediate security does not try to defend him. I realise Alina already owns the whole team of Russians in the room.

"50,000 volts, but only for a sub-second," breathes Christina.

Alina, in English, explains, "Kovarin is finished. He was about to give away a large piece of the obschak in return for a bad deal containing a faulty product.

"I don't know whether you realise Christopher Law, but we know that FST's Akiru system doesn't work. Your late father was trying to sell us a defective product, although maybe your newness in this situation makes you less complicit.

She stares at Kovarin, "Kovarin knew that Akiru didn't work. He could still have made much money from the deal before 'disappearing.' "

She continues to look angrily at Kovarin, now tended by the two bulky paramedics. I work out that the phone call a minute or two earlier must have come from someone high in the Kremlin. I realise that feeding a story about the defective system to Bettina Kübler must have worked and she must have told others.

Alina continues, "I am to send Kovarin back to Moscow, where he will be questioned. Christopher Law and the rest of you must leave us enough room for us to make our departure, and that way you will avoid reprisals."

She made a hand signal of what looked like a cowboy lassoing a steer, and the paramedics manhandle the still slumped Kovarin and load him onto a bright orange collapsible ambulance stretcher. I'd noticed it in a corner of the room when we walked in, but assumed it was some part of the emergency first-aid set up for the high-profile meeting. I see them use securing belts on the stretcher, which run right across Kovarin's bulky body. The head of security gestures for the group to leave Magister Grange, complete with Kovarin on a stretcher.

I can see Christina has reached into her bag. She is still on high alert and, I assume, is preparing a firearm in case it is needed.

Alina speaks to Christopher, "You know, I'm sure, that the deal is off. You will show us all graciously to the helicopters now, as if our meeting has concluded. Try nothing heroic, just remember, you can all get out of this without a scratch."

She gestures to Christopher who looks stunned at what has just happened, but he calmly escorts them to the door of the Grand Saloon and past the busy police officers, who stand out of the way of the apparent dignitaries as they walk outside to the sunlight and the pathway to the helicopter positions. They observe the wheeled stretcher but can see it is now flanked by what appears to be paramedics.

"Minor emergency," is the phrase being used. I can also see hand gestures being made. It's the one that looks like someone having a drink and the flat-palmed wobbly hand one. To an Englishman it implied, 'He had too many drinks and fell over.' I could also hear the expression 'diabetik' being used. They had rehearsed this 'get-out'.

As the last of them leave the Grand Saloon, Chuck presses a small button clipped to his belt. Within seconds the room is filled with British marines who I decide must have come from the base along the coast. They have entered the room through the secret passage.

"Nothing to see," explains Chuck to their commanding officer, "The business concluded peacefully."

I can hear a noise from outside of Magister Grange. I realise it isn't helicopters, but more likely to be military transport vehicles.

"The PPVs have arrived," says Chuck, grinning. He walks to a window and pulls back the shutter. I can make out a short row of sand coloured trucks outside.

"Nice," says Chuck, "Foxhounds and Huskies. This is a well-provisioned area for British Protected Patrol Vehicles."

We make our way to the exit from the Grand Saloon, accompanied by various well-equipped military men. I look at the expressions on DCI Penrose and DI Trewella's faces as they see the outcome of a conjuring trick where about twenty people enter an empty room and then forty walk out.

There is no sign of the Russians, who by now must be over by the helipad.

DCI Penrose calls to us:

"Jake Lambers and Clare Crafts, over here, please!"

We follow the instruction, although I notice Chuck continues to walk toward the helipad.

"What the hell has been happening?" asks Trewella.

"Things got a little lively inside the room," explains Clare, "So the Russians decided to go back to Moscow. Our good friends from the neighbourhood military base decided to provide moral support and have now brought their transports around so that they don't have to walk back.

"But what about the drug ring?" asks Penrose, "Did we find out anything new?"

"It was a massive set-up," explains Clare, "The

Russians were using Abigail Holbrook's drug deal as bait for something else. They created the deal and then leaked it so that British customs would impound the cargo. Holbrook's payment for the drugs was stolen by the Russians. By pressurising Holbrook, they could put a squeeze on Christopher Law. Or so they thought."

"So, the Russians were smuggling the drugs?" asks Trewella. He looks confused.

"Only indirectly," explains Clare, "Abigail Holbrook was trying to climb the slippery ladder by trading far greater quantities of cocaine. Except she paid for the goods in advance, but then had them impounded by customs agencies. She lost around £200k in the process."

"She was running a ring which included Roger Ackroyd - with his supply of four-wheel-drive vehicles and Nat Retallick, who has access to the water with a variety of small rental craft. If you arrest them now, I think they will all fold fairly easily."

"So we will have broken a drugs ring operating from close to Magister Grange?" queried Trewella.

"Not only that, you'll also be able to show it had links to Russia, right back into the Moscow mafia," answers Clare.

*Sonic boom*

There was a loud noise from behind the vineyard. The first of the green Russian/Turkish helicopters was taking off. It was as noisy as hell, but then the second one took off and I thought I was experiencing some kind of military fly past.

"Those Kamovs are so loud," said Christina," They put them in the air first so that the big Mil will have cover when it takes off. The UK could scramble a couple of Lightning F-35s from Swanwick and be all over them in minutes. The F-35s can fly at over 1,200 mph over water."

"Why over water?" I ask.

"Sonic boom!" explains Christina, "And their top speed is classified as well. They are truly a networked plane and can hunt in packs."

Although we are standing maybe 100 metres from

the helipads, we still wince as the big blue Mil starts up and the lifts from the grassy area.

"They won't intercept, however tempting!" says Chuck, almost shouting, from behind us, "It's more useful for everyone if Kovarin gets home to Moscow. Think about it. Kovarin is in disgrace. Everyone thinks Jago Fox is dead. The FST deal is off. People believe the Ikiru doesn't work. Even the drugs ring has been rounded up. Contrast that with shooting down a Russian helicopter on a Turkish flag in British airspace. I don't think so!"

"We'll have to let Penrose and Trewella take the credit for the drug ring capture," says Clare, "And it will make life so much easier for Magister Grange to be freed from the innuendo of drug rings and other speculations!"

We all look out across the River Exe. All three helicopters are now in flight, heading slowly towards the sea.

*London*

We are back in the different noises of Hays Galleria, London. At the Triangle offices.

"A different river," says Clare, looking out of the window, "So much narrower than the Exe."

"Around here it is, you should take a look at Southend!" I answer.

"Are we going along to meet Amanda then?" asks Christina, "I imagine Chuck will be there as well, and I won't be surprised to see Jago and Emmanuelle!"

We've a meeting booked at Amanda's offices along the Thames, in early afternoon. A kind of conclusion to the event of the last few days.

"The taxi's arrived," says Christina, "We'd better go."

We look at this all-electric black cab and think wistfully of the blue Tesla saloons used around Exeter. At least we know the battery technology is in safe hands after the Exeter convention.

"Side gate?" asks the taxi driver.

We all nod. It's amusing to think that Vauxhall Cross headquarters of the British Secret Service has a 'side gate' that all the taxi drivers know about. A bit like 'the steps' at Waterloo and 'the hole in the wall.'

We are soon there and have been escorted through the varied security checks. Once again we are in one of the 'good' boardrooms, just past the broom-cupboard door with '007' written on it.

"Hello!" says Amanda, as we enter the room. I see Jago, Emmanuelle, and Chuck around the table. We do the hugs and as usual Amanda is straight down to business.

"I cannot thank you enough," she opens, "This was above and beyond. Chuck told me about your respective parts in this. Well played, all of you."

"We think we worked it out," says Clare, "You got us invited so that you had some eyes on what was happening. Jago had been embedded with you ever since Cambridge and had told Emmanuelle some of his role. Then the story about the sale of FST came up as bait for the Russians. "

"Right, so far, although the Russians had also created the situation with Abigail Holbrook so that she lost her money and her consignment. It was supposed to be a trigger for the events that unfolded."

"Yes, but Jago stuck to his guns about not wanting to sell," says Clare, "Which created something of an impasse."

"Yes, I had to tread carefully," explains Jago, "If I made it look too easy they would sense a trap. I hadn't expected them to want to remove me though. My undercover role worked a bit too well."

"Yes, so the front man buying the company, Antonovich, arranges a hit on you. By that half-wit Ian Salterton."

"Yes, but luckily I'd been tipped off by Christopher, so I could arrange my disappearance ahead of the attempt on my life. Then Amanda brought in 'Doctor Ellis' to verify my demise and get me moved out of Magister Hall quickly."

"It looked pretty convincing to me," said Clare, "Although none of it made any sense!"

"Well, I was already in London by the time the police were investigating the thing as if it was suspicious."

Amanda speaks, "That's when I had to fly down to Exeter and explain to the police that this was a special intelligence operation and for you, Clare, and Jake to assist. I also told them I was sending Chuck along."

"The police continued to think the main investigation was linked to the drug dealing, and they never discovered that Jago's death had been faked," says Clare.

I was thinking how exhausting it had been to keep the parallel truths alive.

"Then we realised Adam Antonovich is really a front for Alina Petrovna. That Alina is clawing her way into ever more powerful positions in the 'Moscow Mafia'," explains Clare.

"The bratva," clarifies Christina. "So we do a good job to sabotage the deal. We make it compelling by hinting at Chinese interest, knowing all along that Jago has structured it with a poison pill clause."

"But the killer blow was the leak about the Ikiru software not working," adds Jago.

"It meant Kovarin was running a deal which needed

huge amounts of money, which he was borrowing from the obschak - 'Moscow Mafia' fund. And that he'd used elite troops when he was in the negotiation. Only Putin can get away with those kind of moves.

"When the Kremlin and the gangsters from Moscow Solntsevskaya mafia discover that Kovarin is using their resources on a stupid deal, they cut up rough. That's when Alina Petronova was asked to take control - effectively usurping the now damaged goods of Kovarin."

"I've never seen a taser used across a boardroom table before," said Christina, "It certainly quietened things down."

"Yes, with Kovarin nullified, it meant all the other pieces of the jigsaw would fall into place. No FST deal. Kovarin out. Jago missing, presumed dead. Drugs ring discovered and arrested. Christopher takes over FST. The Chinese discover what's happened and back away."

"And Jago and I make our escape back to Canada!" says Emmanuelle.

Then there's some noise, and a dark-suited woman enters the room.

"A Russian package to the Triangle Offices was

intercepted," she says.

We open it. It is flight tickets. Open returns to Istanbul. From Alina.

An inconclusive list of suspects (feel free to make notes)

## UNLIKELY

- Jake Lambers - Me (from The Triangle)
- Clare Crafts – my friend (from The Triangle)

## FAMILY AND RELATED

- Emmanuelle Catteau - inheritor of Seymour House (close to Magister Grange)
- Hans Catteau - first husband of Emmanuelle Catteau (RIP)
- Jago Fox - owner of Magister Grange (site of the party)
- Sadie Fox – Jago's sister-in-law
- Mrs. Cecilia Fox, widow of Hans' ne'er-do-well younger brother
- Katie Law - RIP ex-wife of Jago.
- Christopher Law – son of Katie, stepson to Jago

## GUESTS

- Moskvin Adam Antonovich - Russian from a money house
- Shmagina Alina Petrovna – Adam's friend
- Amelia Brophy - mystery woman - party organiser
- Bettina Kübler - Swiss researcher, at Brant, Geneva, working on eDefense.
- Stéphane Gérard, a very close friend of Bettina.
- Hubert Tempelmann - CTO for Zillian car company
- Alec Haynes - Pop star - Drax

- Joshua Harper (Canadian) - Erebus band member - knows Emmanuelle
- Jallie T – pop star and friend of Clare
- Rishi – Jallie T's bf and gig organiser
- Ian Salterton - A well-known local book author
- Lawrence Booth - A politician (used to live in the area and is returning).
- Bianca Hart - Stunning escort of Lawrence Booth
- Dr Ellis - MD to the family

## NEIGHBOURS

- Melissa Woodmanton - owner of Woodmanton Investments
- Gabriel Woodmanton
- Antonio Campbell - Retired, but owns Milbury Moorings
- Mary Campbell
- Roger Ackroyd - runs 4WD adventure tours of area
- Nat Retallick - runs boating holidays around the River Exe
- Rose Marsh - Runs Post Office
- Penelope Richards - Local landowner and viticulturist
- DCI Morwen Penrose (she/her) – police investigator
- DI Tristan Trewella (he/his) – police investigator

## STAFF AT MAGISTER GRANGE

*Permanent*

- Pascal Duret - butler
- Abigail Holbrook: head of housekeeping / mistress to Jago
- Mrs Margaret Mason (cook)

*Temporary/contract*

- Faith Hudson (parlourmaid)
- Maisy Gill (second housemaid / student)
- Lily Graham: (housemaid)
- Zoe Demelza (kitchen maid / student)
- Robin Duggan (gardener)

Printed in Great Britain
by Amazon

23010343R00169